MISSION: HER SECURITY

TEAM 52 #3

ANNA HACKETT

Mission: Her Security

Published by Anna Hackett

Copyright 2018 by Anna Hackett

Cover by Melody Simmons of BookCoversCre8tive

Cover image by Paul Henry Serres

Edits by Tanya Saari

ISBN (ebook): 978-1-925539-60-8

ISBN (paperback): 978-1-925539-61-5

Beneath a Trojan Moon – SFR Galaxy Award Winner and RWAus Ella Award Winner

Hell Squad – SFR Galaxy Award for best Post-Apocalypse for Readers who don't like Post-Apocalypse

The Anomaly Series – #1 Amazon Action Adventure Romance Bestseller

"Like Indiana Jones meets Star Wars. A treasure hunt with a steamy romance." – SFF Dragon, review of *Among Galactic Ruins*

"Strap in, enjoy the heat of romance and the daring of this group of space travellers!" – Di, Top 500 Amazon Reviewer, review of *At Star's End*

"Action, danger, aliens, romance – yup, it's another great book from Anna Hackett!" – Book Gannet Reviews, review of *Hell Squad: Marcus*

Sign up for my VIP mailing list and get your *free box set* containing three action-packed romances.

Visit here to get started:
www.annahackettbooks.com

CHAPTER ONE

S he was running for her life.

Kinsey Beck's bare feet slapped on the pavement of the dirty alley. Night closed in all around her, massive warehouses looming in the darkness.

Her gut told her she was likely still in Las Vegas, in some industrial area, but she had no real idea where her captors had taken her. They'd hit her so hard when they snatched her that she'd blacked out.

She held back the sob trying to well up in her chest. Her face was one massive throb, and she could only see out of one eye...barely. The other was swollen closed.

A sharp pain speared through her foot. Kinsey winced, but kept running. There were no lights on in any of the warehouses. No opportunities for sanctuary. Just locked roller doors and barred windows. The only sound she could hear was the echo of her harsh breathing.

A shout sounded behind her and her pulse spiked. They were coming.

She pushed for more speed, ignoring the rough ground biting into her feet. She'd known the potential hazards when she'd taken her job. Working for a covert, black ops team carried some risk, even when she was simply an office manager. She ran logistics for Team 52 here in Las Vegas. Her office was a squat, concrete building called the Bunker, out in a quiet corner of McCarran Airport.

She was no one special. Unlike the badasses of Team 52, she didn't carry an assault rifle, or fly off to rescue people, or safeguard and secure pieces of ancient technology.

That was why the team existed. After signing a stack of confidentiality agreements, she'd learned the historians had some things wrong. In the past, humans had been more advanced than most people knew, and had developed some fascinating, and often dangerous, technology.

When one of those artifacts resurfaced, Team 52 came in.

Kinsey was proud of her job, loved what she did.

Dragging in air, she rounded a corner. *Keep running, Kinsey.*

She'd escaped Sugarview, Tennessee, and the trailer she'd grown up in, her drunken daddy, and her bitter, dried-up mama. Kinsey had come to the bright lights of Las Vegas with dreams of being a showgirl. A star, with her name up in lights.

Except she'd been two inches too short. So what if her dreams had been crushed? She was a survivor. She certainly hadn't been planning to go back to Tennessee. There was nothing there for her anymore.

She stumbled over something in the dark alley and almost fell, but quickly righted herself. Like she always did, she picked herself up and kept moving forward.

Instead of heading home with her tail between her legs, she'd worked hard and eventually found a job she loved. A team she loved working with. Especially one big, tall, rugged former Navy SEAL and mountain man.

The voices behind her were getting louder. Her throat tightened.

"There she is!"

Kinsey sucked back another sob. *Faster. Go faster.*

Then she tripped.

She crashed to the ground, falling onto her knees and hands. Her palms scraped on the rough pavement, and she felt blood trickling down one knee.

She leaped up. She had to keep running.

Then she heard noises ahead of her. Was that music? A burst of adrenaline filled her, and she barreled around another corner and onto a wider street.

Ahead, she spotted a bar nestled in among the industrial buildings. It looked pretty rough, but there was light spilling out from a grimy window. A row of Harleys was parked out front.

She sprinted toward the door. Definitely a biker bar.

She was only feet away from the door when arms closed around her from behind and lifted her off the ground.

No! She fought and kicked.

She saw people inside glance up and look out. Grizzled, bearded faces. No one came to help her.

"Settle down," a man's voice ground in her ear.

Hell, no. Instead, she fought harder.

"Quit it." A fist slammed into her head.

Pain exploded and Kinsey cried out. Dazed, she sagged against her captor. The man turned, and she spotted a second man standing in the shadows.

A second later, she was tossed over a hard shoulder. The men began walking back to the warehouse she'd just escaped from.

Dejection filled her. She was trapped, and it didn't matter how much she fought, she couldn't escape.

The thought reminded her of something her mama had repeatedly told her—that she'd never break free, never get away.

You may have inherited my looks, girl, but you're a Beck. Good for nothing. Going nowhere. You'll end up some man's punching bag, alone and shriveled up.

Kinsey closed her eyes. Well, technically eye, singular since one was already swollen shut. Panic clawed at her chest, and instantly her mind went to the one thing that soothed her, comforted her.

The man of her dreams. Smith Creed.

Big, quiet Smith. Six foot four, broad shoulders, trim hips, long, long legs.

Her muscles relaxed a little. He was usually in jeans, ones so faded that they cupped his firm ass lovingly, and made a woman look and fantasize. He had dirty-blond hair—thick hair with strands of so many different colors. She'd tried to name them all—brown, gold, platinum, whiskey, honey, chestnut, wheat, chocolate. He also had a sexy beard that was shades darker than his hair. She often wondered what it would feel like against her skin.

Smith was everything Kinsey had ever wanted. A strong man, with a code, who fought for his country. A man who would never get sloppy drunk, knock a woman around, or shout at a kid.

Of course, he wasn't interested in her. She got it. He was tough, gorgeous, and badass, and had spent his life protecting others.

She was nothing.

The men stepped back into the warehouse, their bootsteps echoing on the concrete.

Lights were on in one corner of the space, with a few camp chairs set up where her captors were playing cards.

The man carrying her set her down, and dragged her through a door and into a small bathroom. It wasn't much. Dirty toilet, single sink, and cracked tiles. She heard the clink of handcuffs and felt the cool steel on her wrist. A second later, he attached the handcuffs to the pipes under the sink and turned to leave.

He paused in the doorway. "You run again, I'll break your legs."

He slammed the door closed behind him, cutting off the light.

And Kinsey sat there in the darkness, alone, on her knees on the dirty tiles.

Looked like her mama was right.

SMITH CREED WAS ANGRY.

He paced the computer room at the Area 52 base. He

hadn't slept much during the two days since Kinsey had been kidnapped.

He turned and stared at the cellphone on the high counter in the center of the room. The bastards who snatched her had left it, along with a note saying that they'd taken her.

They'd also said they'd call with their demands. So why the fuck hadn't they called?

A muscle ticked in his jaw and he wrestled with the urge to punch something.

Fuck.

He pivoted, well aware that his teammates were watching him warily. His team leader Lachlan was staying close, prepared to contain him if he lost his shit. His teammate Axel wasn't far away, either. The former Special Forces Marine and Army Delta Force soldiers could probably take Smith together. Not to mention, one of Lachlan's arms was a high-tech prosthetic—strong and deadly. But Smith was big, well-trained, and mad as fuck. It would be messy.

Smith started pacing again. He was trying hard to keep his anger under control. But his damn head kept torturing him with images of what might be happening to Kinsey. Sweet, delicate Kinsey. Always smiling that megawatt smile that could stop traffic. Shit, if they'd hurt one strand of blonde hair on her head...

Brooks, their computer geek and comms guru, groaned and leaned against the counter. He looked exhausted. He'd been running searches for two days straight, trying to work out who had taken Kinsey. The man's rumpled T-shirt had a picture of Darth Vader on it, with the words "Warning, choking hazard" written beneath the image. Brooks dropped his chin into his hand, the tattoos on his muscular arm flexing. He might be a geek, but the former Navy Intelligence officer was fit and in shape.

Data scrolled across all the screens on the wall. Brooks had searches going all over the place. Smith had spent several hours helping Brooks comb through the Bunker's security footage.

But they hadn't found anything that had helped them. The men who snatched her had come prepared, wearing balaclavas and using a stolen car they'd later abandoned. There was nothing on video that could identify them.

Images of the Bunker flashed like photos through Smith's brain. The overturned furniture, the files strewn around, the blood on the carpet.

"Why haven't they called?" Smith growled. He needed action, craved it.

He'd grown up in the Colorado mountains, hunting and tracking with his dad. Smith preferred being outdoors. He preferred *doing*, not sitting on his ass waiting.

"Patience." Lachlan was always the voice of reason.

"Fuck patience." Smith kicked the counter.

Axel crossed his arms, leaning against the wall. "We're going to find her."

"Not sitting around here, we won't," Smith ground out.

7

The computer room doors slid open, and a tall, African-American man strode in, his white lab coat flowing around his muscular body. Dr. Ty Sampson ran the lab at the base. The former DARPA scientist had short, dark hair, a goatee, and a genius-level IQ. He also had an ornery personality, was a medical doctor as well, and spent most of his time inventing cutting-edge tech for the team to use.

Lachlan straightened. "What have you got, Ty?"

"The blood at the Bunker wasn't Kinsey's."

"She fought back." Smith's lips curved into a smile. She had to have been scared, but she'd fought them. Then his smile faded. But she wasn't a trained soldier. She could have been hurt in the process.

All of a sudden, the cellphone on the counter top rang.

They all froze. Smith stared at it, his heart pounding.

The doors opened again and two athletic women ran inside. The taller woman was Team 52's second in command, Blair. Her blonde ponytail swinging behind her and her tank top displayed her toned arms. Beside her, their team medic Callie was dark to Blair's light. With her Native Hawaiian heritage, she had straight, black hair and a slimmer build.

Blair charged forward and grabbed Smith's hand. He met her gaze—one blue eye and one silver prosthetic. She was as tough as nails, but she had a soft spot that she kept well protected. He knew she was just as worried about Kinsey as he was.

Lachlan nodded at Brooks.

Brooks swiped something on his tablet, then touched the phone.

"We have something that belongs to you." The voice sounded like a robot, altered by a voice changer.

Brooks tapped his tablet's screen, no doubt scrambling to trace the call.

"Is Kinsey okay?" Lachlan asked.

"She's alive. If you want her to stay that way, you need to do exactly as we instruct."

Lachlan pressed his hands to the counter. "We're listening." His voice was calm, but Smith knew him well enough to know that his boss was pissed.

"You will deliver a device to us. In return, we will give you the woman."

Smith clenched his teeth together so hard he was sure his jaw was about to crack. The woman. Like she was just a fucking bargaining chip.

"I want proof that she's alive," Smith said.

Lachlan shot him an annoyed look.

"Don't listen to them." Kinsey's voice. "Don't give them anything!"

Smith surged forward, like he could reach through the phone and grab her. Blair and Axel gripped his arms, holding him back.

"We want an artifact that was recovered from Tibet," the robot voice intoned.

Lachlan's head snapped up. "I don't know what—"

"You do know, Commander Hunter. Don't play games with us. Bring it to the Pinnacle Industrial Park in Las Vegas. Warehouse 112. You have exactly twelve hours, or we'll kill her."

The line went dead.

Lachlan spun. "Brooks? You trace the call?"

The man shook his head. "Wasn't long enough."

"Check out that address," Lachlan ordered.

"Already on it."

Lachlan speared Smith with a sharp look. "You got a grip, Creed?"

"No." Smith breathed deeply. "But I'm holding. I want Kinsey back."

Something worked through Lachlan's golden eyes. "You and Kinsey—?"

Smith shook his head. "I just want her back safely."

"It's all right, big guy," Blair said. "We've all seen you watching her."

Smith had watched Lachlan and their other teammate Seth fall in love recently. Seth was still on his honeymoon. The team had given both men a lot of good-natured shit about it. They all had fucking happy endings in their heads.

But Smith knew not everyone got happy endings. His bitch of an ex-wife had seared that particular lesson into him.

"I want Kinsey back safely, that's all." That's all he'd let it be.

"Got the address," Brooks said. "The industrial park is in northern Vegas. Near Nellis Air Force Base. Warehouse is empty. Up for lease."

"What's this artifact?" Axel asked.

Lachlan sighed. "I have no fucking clue. Do you know how many things are stored in the warehouse? Some from well before our time. Call Nat in."

Moments later, there was the click of heels outside, and a dark-haired woman entered. The Team 52 archeologist, Dr. Natalie Blackwell, always looked like she'd just stepped off a catwalk. Today, her fitted skirt was red, and her shirt a creamy white. Her black hair fell smoothly over her shoulders, framing a face that hinted at Asian ancestry.

"You got a call?" Her voice held a soft Australian accent. "Is Kinsey okay?"

"She's alive," Lachlan said. "Kidnappers want a device from Tibet."

Nat's face tightened.

"What is it?" Smith asked.

"It's a sound-producing device. It looks like an instrument."

"Pretty sure these assholes don't want to make music," Smith said.

"It's ancient levitation technology," Nat said.

Smith crossed his arms. "It's what?"

"Tibetan monks have known for centuries how to use sound to levitate large objects."

"Shit, this job never gets old," Axel muttered. "I'll say the obligatory 'you can't be serious?'"

Nat shot him a look. "There are several ancient documents that talk about past civilizations using sound to move large blocks. It's been a theory on how the Egyptians managed to build things as vast as the pyramids for years."

Axel snorted. "But it's wrong, right?" He straightened. "Right? They used mud ramps."

Nat lifted a slim shoulder. "We don't know. There

are plenty of theories, but a mud ramp large enough to build the Great Pyramid would have to have been several times larger than the pyramid itself, and an engineering feat all of its own."

Axel leaned against the bench. "Damn."

"Levitation is a real thing?" Blair asked.

Nat nodded. "Acoustic levitation is very real. Utilizing the correct sound waves, you can suspend an object in the air. I could go into detail about standing waves, and nodes—"

Lachlan held up a hand. "Please don't."

A grin flickered briefly over the archeologist's face. "NASA's been experimenting with anti-gravity for years. Scientists in Japan successfully levitated a metal screw. Scientists in France have levitated droplets of water. In China, a team managed to levitate small animals—ants and tiny fish—without harming them."

"Okay, so only small stuff," Lachlan said.

"Right. But, our more advanced ancestors knew how to levitate much larger things," Nat added. "Like blocks of stone weighing tons. I've read an account by an Arabic historian describing the ancient Egyptians using a metal rod to strike stone, create sound, and levitate large rocks."

"Wow," Callie murmured.

"Even in the Bible, it mentions the sound of trumpets bringing down the walls of Jericho."

"So, the Tibetan device?" Smith prompted.

"The knowledge of sound levitation was passed down and protected by monks in Tibet. In the 1930s, a Swedish doctor was visiting in Tibet. The monks allowed him to witness them using instruments to levitate huge rocks up a cliff face. Hundreds of feet up." Nat tucked a strand of dark hair back behind her ear. "We have one of those devices. Unfortunately, the Swedish doctor shared his amazing experience with others, and it was about the same time that a certain man in Germany had pseudo-archeologists searching the world for ancient objects of power."

"Shit," Lachlan said.

Nat nodded. "Yes. The Nazis made a play to get their hands on the levitation devices, but the U.S. government sent a team in to protect the monks. The monks hid or destroyed their instruments, and gave one to the U.S. team."

"So it's dangerous?" Blair asked.

"It could be," Nat answered. "Depending how it's used."

Smith looked back at the screens. "And we have no idea who these bastards are?"

"How the hell do they know about us?" Blair added, frowning. "And the artifact."

"Will Grayson approve the trade?" Smith asked Lachlan.

Jonah Grayson was the Director of Team 52. His background was a bit of a mystery, but Smith knew the guy wore a suit like a second skin, and navigated Washington politics like a pro. Still, something about the man told Smith that he could handle himself in a back alley as well.

Lachlan drew in a deep breath. "No chance in hell."

Smith cursed. "So, we just throw Kinsey under a fucking bus."

"I didn't say that—"

"I won't approve handing a dangerous piece of ancient technology over to criminals," a deep voice drawled.

Smith turned his head and watched the man himself stride into the room.

The big boss wore dark trousers and a snow-white shirt that Smith suspected cost as much as Smith's entire wardrobe of jeans and T-shirts. He had coal-black hair, piercing green eyes, bronze skin, and a sharp face Smith guessed women would find appealing.

Smith's hands curled into fists.

"But I will approve a rescue mission," Jonah said.

Air shuddered out of Smith.

The director looked at Ty. "You have six hours to create a reasonable copy of the artifact, then we need to prepare to get back to Las Vegas."

A wide smile broke out on Ty's face. "You're going to trade a fake for Kinsey." The scientist nodded. "I'm on it."

Smith relaxed a bit. It was risky, but it could work. He'd make it work.

"We have an incoming call," Brooks called out. "Las Vegas Metropolitan Police."

Beside Smith, Blair stiffened. "Shit."

A man's rugged face appeared on the screen. He wore a black shirt, and had a shiny badge hanging from a chain around his neck. The police detective was their contact at LVMPD.

"Detective MacKade," Jonah drawled.

"Director Grayson." MacKade's brown gaze moved

across the room, lingering for a second on Blair, before he zeroed in on Lachlan.

"I have intel for you. Last night, some bikers reported a woman running from two men at a bar in northern Las Vegas. Rough area. Mainly industrial."

Smith straightened. "Anyone help her?"

"Shit," the detective muttered. "So, she is yours. From the description, I guessed."

"Did anyone help her?" Smith repeated, a little louder.

MacKade shook his head. "My informant was an undercover cop. He's been undercover with a biker gang for months. The bikers had no interest in wading in, and my man couldn't risk blowing his cover."

Smith gritted his teeth and slammed a fist onto the counter. "So they fucking left her."

"Smith." Lachlan waited a beat. "We have a recovery plan. You know who these guys were?"

MacKade shook his head.

"You get any more sightings, we'd appreciate a heads-up," Lachlan said.

MacKade nodded, then hesitated. "My guy said she'd been beaten up pretty badly. He barely held out from going after the guys who nabbed her. Said she was fighting them."

Smith looked down at his boots, sucking in air. Kinsey beaten, fighting for her life.

"Thanks for the info." Jonah inclined his head.

"Good luck," MacKade said. "Bring her home." He ended the video call.

"I'll get to work on the artifact decoy." Ty headed for the door.

Nat rose to follow. "I'll help."

Smith raised his head, his gaze hitting Lachlan's. He wanted to get out there. He wanted Kinsey back.

Lachlan nodded. "We have a rescue mission to plan."

CHAPTER TWO

S mith checked his weapons for probably the tenth time. First, he went over his high-tech, CXM7 rifle. It wasn't just an assault rifle, but also had an integrated grenade launcher and shotgun. Next, he checked his grenades, then his SIG Sauer. Finally, he added a few grenades to the pockets on his vest.

He was already wearing his all-black tactical gear. He was in the team locker room, the rest of the team around him, all prepping for the mission. Everyone's faces were set and focused.

I'm coming, Kinsey. Hold on.

Smith slammed his locker door closed. He'd actually managed a short nap while Ty worked to make the decoy artifact. He knew that Kinsey needed him focused and alert, not exhausted. He sat on the metal bench between the lockers and lifted the left leg of his cargo pants up.

He triple-checked his high-tech prosthetic. On his last mission as a SEAL, things had gotten fucked. Beyond recognition. That included Smith's left foot. He'd still managed to drag an unconscious, bleeding teammate to their extraction point. But afterward, he'd lost his foot and ankle.

And for a while, Smith had thought his life was over. He'd spent a year having surgery, physical therapy, drinking, and feeling pretty damn sorry for himself. Until Team 52 had come knocking, with a second chance to do what he was good at.

And the chance for Ty to fit him with a prosthetic that was integrated into Smith's nervous system and was almost better than the foot he'd lost.

Smith lowered his pant leg, stood, and swung his rifle onto his shoulder. He slid his SIG into his thigh holster, and then headed out of the locker room. Soon, the entire team—minus Seth—regrouped in the rec room.

Ty arrived, carrying a large, black, metal box. Beside him was the head of the warehouse storage facility, Arlo Green. The older, grizzled, former military man was carrying a matching black box. The men set the boxes on a table and opened them.

Smith studied the artifacts—both real and fake. They looked like small, solid-looking trumpets made of a silver metal. They started out narrow, flaring out to a wider end. He couldn't tell them apart.

"This artifact's been stored here a long time." Arlo pointed to the real thing. "From before the team was even put together."

It was incredible to think that this thing could lift stones weighing tons into the air. Still, Smith had seen some mind-blowing things since he'd been recruited for Team 52.

"Good job, Ty," Lachlan said.

The scientist shrugged. "I am a genius."

Blair nodded. "They look identical to me."

"They try to test it, and it ain't gonna levitate shit." Arlo's voice sounded like gravel, as he closed the case.

Lachlan nodded. "We'll be long gone with Kinsey before they try to do that." He looked at the team, grabbing the handles on the case. "Let's move out."

Finally. Smith was edgy, eager. He headed into the elevator, and soon they were zooming up to the surface.

Axel brushed his fingers over his rifle. "About damn time."

They wasted no time exiting the aircraft hangar and heading to their experimental jet helicopter. The X8 was a sleek, gray aircraft with the wide body and jet engines of a plane, and the dual co-axial rotors of a helicopter. It was fast, maneuverable, and had a long range.

Lachlan loaded the box in the storage area at the back of the X8. Then they all climbed in the side door, settling into the seats. Blair moved to the cockpit. She and Seth were the team pilots. Today, she'd be flying solo.

Smith sat back in his seat, his hands resting on his rifle.

Lachlan grabbed an overhead handhold, his face intense. "Let's bring Kinsey home."

They would. Smith was going to ensure she was safe and secure.

Moments later, the X8 lifted off, moving smoothly

into the air. They swept out over the desert, heading toward Las Vegas.

Lachlan touched his ear. They all wore state-of-the-art microdot earpieces. "Go ahead, Brooks."

Smith watched, waiting to hear the update.

Lachlan nodded. "Thanks." He looked at Smith, Axel, and Callie. "Brooks studied the satellite feed and had Nellis send up a drone. Warehouse is empty, and he's not picking up any heat signatures. So, it doesn't look like they have an ambush planned."

Smith frowned. "No heat signatures? Then where's Kinsey?"

Lachlan shrugged a shoulder. "Likely they'll move her into position just before the deadline."

Smith pulled in a breath. In just a few hours, they'd have her back.

Shifting into a seat, Lachlan raised his voice. "We'll go to—"

All of a sudden, alarms blared from the cockpit. Lachlan jumped to his feet. "Mason?"

"Fuck," Blair shouted. "We have a missile incoming!"

Missile. Smith's body went stiff.

"Evasive maneuvers," Lachlan yelled.

"Strap in," Blair shouted back.

Lachlan dived into his seat, strapping in. The jet-copter veered sharply left, throwing Smith back against his chair. He gripped the armrests. He generally liked flying, but he hated when things got rough.

The X8 veered to the right, and he heard Axel mutter a curse in Spanish. Blair was shouting from the cockpit as she worked to avoid the missile.

Boom.

The aircraft shuddered under the impact, then started to spin.

"We're hit," Blair yelled.

Smith gritted his teeth, the X8 whirling in a sickening death spiral. He turned his head to look out the window. Flames and smoke were rising from the wing. Beyond that, lay the broad expanse of brown desert.

"Brace positions," Blair called out.

"Fuck," Axel bit out from behind Smith.

Smith braced, but all he could think about was Kinsey. That smiling, beautiful face. He'd had a chance at that piece of heaven, and he'd stupidly pushed her away.

The X8 hit the desert sand.

Metal crunched and glass broke.

Smith was thrown hard against his harness and something glanced off his head. Everything went black.

KINSEY DREW her knees up to her chest, the handcuff on her wrist clanking against the pipes she was cuffed to. At least it was only one wrist. Still, the wrist was red and raw from her attempts to escape.

They'd moved her hours ago. She'd been shuffled into a blacked-out truck, driven for hours, and was now in some sort of dilapidated cabin. From the glimpse she'd gotten when her captors had yanked her out of the truck, they were somewhere in the desert.

It was quiet. No city sounds. No cars driving past. Nothing.

She grabbed the warm soda beside her and took a sip. It wasn't much, but the soda and potato chips they'd given her to eat was better than nothing.

Her face was still throbbing, but she mostly ignored it. She sat back in her shadowed corner of an empty room she guessed was a bedroom. As far as she could tell, the rustic cabin only had three rooms—the living room with a modest kitchen, a tiny bathroom, and the room she was in. Surreptitiously, she looked through the open doorway.

Two of her four captors were sitting at a rickety table in the living area.

She'd never seen any of them before, and she'd done her best to memorize their faces. She knew there were others, as she'd heard them talking on the phone. From what she could tell, most of them were Italian-American, with bronze skin, dark hair, and American accents. They reminded her of the man she'd had a couple of unfortunate dates with a few weeks back. He'd had the same dark good looks. Shame they'd hidden a pushy, cloying personality.

The oldest of the group had dark, curly hair and black eyes, and appeared to be the boss. She'd nicknamed him Mr. Big.

Mr. Short was about her height, with a thin, scrawny body. He looked strung out and excited by everything.

Mr. Stocky was buff, with no neck. He looked like he spent too much time in the gym. He had a tattoo down his arm of some sort of snake, and from what she could tell, he looked like he was ex-military. She'd gotten pretty good at picking out who was military after working with Team 52.

Mr. Cool smiled all the time, and had even, handsome features. He thought pretty highly of himself. His curly hair flopped over his forehead, almost into his velvet-brown eyes, and a dashing scar bisected one eyebrow.

Mr. Big and Mr. Stocky had gone out at least an hour ago, super excited about something. She knew they were keeping in touch via a radio with the pair who stayed with her.

The radio on the table flared to life. "Base, this is Rover. Bingo! The bird is down."

The two men at the table grinned and started cheering.

Kinsey licked her lips and strained to hear more. What was going on now?

"Fucking hotshots aren't so hot when their fancy helicopter is in pieces on the desert sand," Mr. Cool boasted. He bumped his knuckles against Mr. Short's.

Kinsey's heart stopped. *No.* They couldn't be talking about Team 52.

Mr. Cool looked her way, smirking. "Our boys just bested your boys."

Bile rose in her throat. She'd held the spark of hope inside her that the team was coming to rescue her.

Now...

She couldn't let herself think about it. She shut her thoughts down. All she had to focus on was getting out of there. If Team 52 had really been taken down, she only had herself to depend on.

Kinsey shifted, and her cuffs rattled against the pipes. She wasn't going anywhere. Despair rose up inside her. She was trapped and helpless. And this was all her fault. If she hadn't fallen for their stupid trick at the Bunker and let them in...

She'd put Team 52 in danger. Smith, Blair, and the others.

Tears pricked her eyes. They couldn't be dead. Big, beautiful Smith couldn't be gone.

The minutes ticked by and she frantically tried to think of something she could do. She stared at the handcuffs. She couldn't do anything cuffed to this darn pipe.

She cleared her throat. "I need to pee."

Mr. Short heaved out an annoyed sigh. He rose, pulling a key from his pocket. He quickly uncuffed her and dragged her toward the bathroom.

"Be quick." He slammed the door shut after her.

In the bathroom, Kinsey eyed the small, grimy window. She tried to open it, but after a few grunts, she realized that it had been painted shut.

A threadbare hand towel hung limply off the rail. She grabbed it and wrapped it around her fist. Swallowing, she punched the glass. To her ears, the breaking sound was loud and her heart hammered like a drum in her ears. God, had they heard it?

No one rushed in.

She carefully knocked more glass out. She had no idea what she'd do once she got out, but she couldn't just sit here and do nothing.

Swallowing, she looked out. There was nothing but

dry, dusty desert surrounding the cabin. God, where the hell would she go?

It didn't matter. One step at a time. Get out, then run. She sized up the window, pressing one foot to the wall. This was going to be tight.

The door flew open.

"Nuh-uh." Mr. Cool grabbed her, yanking her out of the room. He flung her and she went flying, falling onto her hands and knees. Cool strode toward her, his handsome face twisted, aggression in every line of his body.

Kinsey jumped up. She was done being the victim.

She'd trained with Team 52. Blair had showed her plenty of moves. Letting that training take over, Kinsey kicked out. She hit Mr. Cool between the legs and he froze, making a pained sound. When he dropped to his knees, she followed with a chop to the back of the head. It reverberated up her arm.

He dropped into the fetal position, groaning.

Mr. Short appeared. "What the fuck?"

Before she could think what to do next, he backhanded her. She flew to the side, her shoulder slamming into the wall. *Ow.*

He grabbed a bunch of her shirt and dragged her back to the empty bedroom where she'd been before. He wasn't gentle when he re-cuffed her to the exposed pipes.

"Bitch." Mr. Cool was back on his feet, doubled over a little. His lips were tight with pain, and he wasn't so cool now.

"Forget it," Short said. "You got bested by a girl. Best to pretend it didn't happen, man."

Cool lifted his chin, his jaw working. "Lucky I'm in a

good mood, seeing as your people are splattered across the desert." He laughed.

The sound grated and Mr. Short joined in. They slammed the door closed, and Kinsey wrapped her arms around herself and curled up in despair.

CHAPTER THREE

S mith opened his eyes and shook his head to clear it. It throbbed. *Fuck.*

He was still strapped to his seat, his shoulders and head aching. He moved, pain shooting through him again, and he groaned.

Shoving down the pain, he looked around, taking in the shattered ruins of the X8. Air whistled through his teeth. *Fuck.* They'd crashed.

He heard a deep groan nearby. "Axel?"

Unclipping his harness, Smith staggered to his feet. He wrenched some wreckage out of the way. He saw Axel's black-clad legs protruding from under a seat. He pulled the seat off his teammate and helped the other man up.

Axel groaned and pressed a hand to his bleeding head. "I know I must be alive. If I was dead, I wouldn't hurt this much."

Smith spotted Lachlan still in his seat. He wasn't moving. *Damn.* Smith glanced at the back of the X8. Callie was sprawled on the floor.

"Help Callie."

Axel nodded and moved. Smith pressed his fingers to Lachlan's throat. The man's pulse was strong and steady. He was alive, but unconscious.

Smith spun to the front of the aircraft. There was too much debris blocking the way to the cockpit. "Blair? Can you hear me?"

No response.

He tugged at the torn metal, but it was wedged in place. "Blair!" Smith touched his ear. "Blair? Brooks? You there?" He waited, hearing deafening silence. "Brooks?"

Nothing.

Smith hoped to hell that Blair was okay. He knew she was as tough as titanium, but they'd crashed hard.

"Callie's got a bump on the back of her head, but she seems okay." Axel had the unconscious Callie slumped in a seat. He was gripping the back of one chair, clutching his CXM.

"Lachlan's out too. No word from Blair and we've got no comms."

"We got shot down." Axel's tone was filled with rage.

Suddenly, Smith heard the sound of a vehicle outside. He and Axel both crouched.

"Here." Axel tossed Smith's CXM at him.

They both whipped their rifles up.

Through a gash in the side of the aircraft, Smith caught a glimpse of a desert dune buggy and a dirt bike, bouncing toward them across the rocky landscape.

"Good Samaritans?" Axel murmured.

Smith's muscles tensed. "I'm guessing no."

The vehicles moved to the back of the X8, out of sight. The engines cut off, and a second later, they heard voices.

Smith pointed and Axel nodded. They both shifted closer to the tear in the metal, clutching their weapons.

They waited. Smith had hunting in his blood. He'd learned the importance of being patient as a kid at his dad's knee.

"Over here, Benny," a man said.

"On it. Let's do this. Enzo's waiting for us to call when it's done."

There were a few minutes of silence, and then Smith heard a banging. Metal striking metal. He tensed. *Fuckers.*

"They're opening the aircraft storage compartment."

Axel's eyes widened and he muttered a curse in Spanish.

These had to be the assholes who brought them down. They were after the artifact.

The assholes who had Kinsey.

Smith pointed to Axel and then to the side door of the X8. He gave another set of hand signals. Axel's jaw tightened, but he nodded. Then Axel gripped the side door.

Smith held up his hand, counting down with his fingers. Then Axel yanked the door open.

It didn't open all the way, but the gap was enough for Smith to slide through. He whipped his weapon up and opened fire.

"Fuck!" a deep voice shouted.

Smith watched the two men dive out of view, hidden by the wreck of the X8. Smith advanced, still firing.

Suddenly, bullets whizzed back at him. He dodged, pressing his back to the side of the aircraft.

He'd gotten a good look at them. Two men in jeans and ball caps, with scarves tied over the bottom half of their faces.

There was nothing about their appearance to give away who they were.

But they had Kinsey. These were the fuckers who'd taken her, hurt her. He wasn't letting them get away.

He glanced over and saw the dune buggy and motorbike parked not too far away. His gaze fell on the RPG launcher resting in the back of the buggy.

Smith's lips firmed. Bastards had signed their own death warrants. But he couldn't kill them until he knew where Kinsey was.

More gunfire broke out, and Smith pulled back. He risked a glance around the X8 and saw the two men racing toward their vehicles.

The artifact box was held between them as they fired random, wild shots behind them.

Smith fired a few shots, careful not to hit them. Axel appeared beside him, raising his CXM.

"No," Smith said. "Let them go."

"What?" Axel looked at him askance.

"We need them to lead us to Kinsey. You stay here, take care of the others, and wait for help."

Smith strode forward.

"Smith, this is not a great plan—"

"Going to get Kinsey back."

He saw the two men toss the box in the dune buggy. He fired a few more shots in their direction, keeping the pressure on. When one of the men broke away, heading for the dirt bike, Smith increased fire, peppering the ground around him with bullets.

The man ducked, abandoned the bike, and ran back towards the buggy. The other man was already pulling away, and the second man dived into the passenger seat.

The buggy sped off, fishtailing in the sand.

Smith sprinted toward the bike. He swung his rifle onto his shoulder and jumped on. A second later, he started the engine, revved it, and sped off.

He gunned the bike, swerving around several scraggly bushes. Ahead, the buggy sent up a cloud of dust.

Smith drove over a small mound of dirt, and the bike launched into the air. He landed, just as bullets whizzed past him. He swerved to the side and started zig-zagging.

When he glanced up, he saw the passenger was holding a gun, firing back at him with one hand. Thankfully, his shots were going wild.

Then suddenly, the man shoved something out of the back of the buggy.

The RPG launcher.

The grenade launcher bounced on the rocky ground and Smith dodged.

His bike skidded out of the control. Gritting his teeth, he fought to keep from crashing. He bounced over some shrubs, his bone rattling. Gunning the engine, he managed to recover.

More bullets flew past him and he leaned low. He swerved again and pulled his SIG out. He held the bike as steady as he could, aimed, and fired.

The man ducked down.

Missed. Smith blew out a breath. The man popped back up, firing again.

Smith carefully took aim. *Bam.*

The man jerked, then flew out the side of the buggy. He hit the desert floor, tumbling over and over.

Smith dodged his body.

The driver didn't stop for his comrade. He kept speeding across the desert landscape that was growing rockier and rockier. Suddenly, the buggy made a sharp turn, and that's when Smith realized they were following a faint track.

He kept following the vehicle, using the dust cloud for cover as much as he could. Minutes ticked by, and then Smith spotted the cabin in the distance. It wasn't much, and he'd seen rough hunting cabins in the mountains of Colorado.

He slowed down, letting the buggy pull ahead. He watched the vehicle speed up to the cabin and skid to a stop in front of it. The driver jumped out, firing in Smith's direction.

Damn. Smith swerved. The shots kept coming, and a bullet clipped him, a searing pain on his bicep.

He swung the bike wide, leaning over the handlebars. He circled around the other side of the cabin. There was a back door.

Then he stopped the bike, leaped off, and swung his CXM off his shoulder.

Kinsey had to be inside.

I'm coming, Kinsey.

He had to get in there before they used her as a shield or formulated a plan. He strode up to the door of the cabin, lifted a boot, and kicked the door open.

The roar of gunfire.

Bullets slammed into the door. Smith swiveled and fired.

A man went down with a scream.

More gunfire. Smith dived across the wooden floor, rolled, and came up firing. But his opponent had dived behind a ratty-assed couch.

Smith yanked a smoke grenade off his belt, activated it, and lobbed it across the room.

Bang. There was a hiss as smoke filled the space.

Smith held his breath and backed up to the front door. He stared down his scope.

He heard coughing, then quiet. The smoke started to dissipate.

Smith strode in.

The man launched himself at Smith. He hit Smith hard, grabbing him around the waist. The bastard was lean, but strong. Smith grunted.

They spun, slamming into the wall with a crack.

The man's eyes were red, and he reared back, throwing a sloppy punch.

Fueled by anger, Smith crashed his fist into the man's gut. With a groan, the man bent over. Smith grabbed him and rammed his head into the wall. The man made an agonized sound, and Smith spun him around, dragging him onto his toes.

"Where is she?" he growled.

The man pressed his lips together.

Smith shook him. "Where. Is. She?"

The man tried to kick Smith, and the sliver of patience Smith was holding onto evaporated. He rammed the man into the wall again.

"You start talking, or I'll take my time breaking every bone in your body."

The man's gaze darted to a nearby doorway.

Smith shoved him backward and followed through with a front kick. His boot struck the man's chest and he flew back, hit the couch, and tipped over it. When he landed in a heap on the floor, he didn't get back up.

Scanning the cabin, Smith searched for any more attackers. He didn't see or sense anyone. He circled the couch and yanked the man off the floor.

The asshole struggled clumsily, but Smith yanked out a zip tie and bound him. He strode over to the first man he'd shot. The man was slumped against the wall, blood oozing from his chest. He rolled pained eyes at Smith but didn't move. Smith zip-tied him as well.

He dragged both men to the ugly kitchen and opened the cupboard under the sink. He then tied them to the pipes beneath.

The roar of an engine sounded outside. With a curse, Smith strode to the window. He saw the dune buggy speeding away, a giant plume of dust behind it.

Fuck. One of them had gotten away with the decoy artifact.

But Smith didn't care. There was something else far more important to him still here in the cabin.

He spun, facing the door to what he guessed was a bedroom.

Mouth dry, not sure what he was going to find, he strode toward it.

CHAPTER FOUR

K insey sat curled on the floor, her free hand digging into her thigh. Her arm was numb from being cuffed for so long, but all she could do was listen to the shouts and gunfire outside the door.

Then everything went silent.

She swallowed, feeling like she had a rock in her throat.

She had no idea what was happening. Had her kidnappers started fighting amongst themselves? Her heart knocked painfully in her chest. She wanted to believe it was Team 52. That they weren't really dead. She closed her eyes and imagined Smith's rugged face. He was the most beautiful man she'd ever seen.

The door handle rattled and the door swung open.

Kinsey sucked in a breath, blinking at the light. Her darn swollen eye didn't help.

She heard a harsh inhalation of breath and she stiffened. Then she felt a big hand on her shoulder and couldn't control her flinch.

No. Her survival instincts kicked in. She was going to fight. She was going to survive.

She tried to kick her attacker, catching him in the calf. She heard a grunt. She knew she couldn't have done much damage, but it felt good.

"Kinsey."

She froze and tipped her head, blinking her one good eye.

Smith was standing there, dressed all in black and covered in a layer of desert dust.

He was breathing and very much alive.

"Smith." Her voice broke.

"I'm here, babe." He crouched down in front of her. His gaze ran over her face, and his lips pressed together. She watched a muscle tick in his jaw. He looked like he was about to lose it.

"Smith," she said again, desperate to know that he wasn't a hallucination.

He pulled something out of his vest and she saw some sort of key in his long fingers. He reached for the handcuffs.

"How are you doing?" His voice was a deep rumble.

"Oh, you know, a little tied up."

Her joke fell flat, and he didn't smile. Not that Smith smiled that much, anyway.

A second later, her arms were free. Kinsey cried out as pins and needles exploded in her limbs. He took one arm in his big hands, rubbing gently.

She was free.

A sob welled and she moved, slamming into his chest. She almost knocked him over as she burrowed against him.

Big, strong arms closed around her.

"I've got you."

Her breath hitched. "You came for me."

"Yeah."

"You came," she whispered again.

"Yeah, Kinsey. You're part of the team." He tugged her closer. "Gonna make sure you're safe and secure."

"They...they told me they shot the X8 down, and that you were all dead."

He paused. "They did bring the X8 down in the desert."

She sucked in a horrified breath.

"I left Axel with the others. I know Lachlan and Callie were alive, just unconscious. I came after you."

Kinsey pulled in a shaky breath, her fingers gripping his vest. She felt the heat pumping off his big body. "Seth? Blair?"

"Seth's still on his honeymoon. I didn't have time to check on Blair before I came for you. But she's fucking tough. She'll be fine."

He'd come after her.

Something inside Kinsey steadied. She was alive. She'd be okay.

She knew that bruises faded, cuts mended, and wounds healed. She'd unfortunately learned that the hard way from her drunken daddy's slaps, and her mama's backhands.

She was Kinsey Mae Beck. She knew how to pull herself up by her bootstraps, and make lemons into lemonade.

"You aren't going to cry, are you?" Smith sounded uncomfortable.

She gave a watery laugh. "You just survived a plane crash and took down all these bad guys single-handedly, and you're afraid of a few tears?"

"Yeah."

She looked up and smiled up at him. "I'll try not to cry."

His big hand stroked over her swollen eye so gently. Anger burned in his eyes.

"I'm okay," she said. "It'll heal."

He moved, sweeping her up into his arms. God, he was so strong. As he carried her out the door, she felt so incredibly tiny.

In the main room, she saw him scowl at the two men tied up in the kitchen. Kinsey glared at them.

"I'll be back for you," Smith growled.

When they stepped outside, Kinsey blinked at the bright sunshine. He carried her over to a motorbike, and set her down. She watched as he swung one long leg over the bike, then he gripped her hand and tugged her closer.

"Climb on," he told her.

Gingerly, she climbed on behind him, settling in.

"Hold tight." He pulled her arms around his middle.

Kinsey leaned in. God, he was so warm and so hard. She pressed her cheek to his back, and heard the bike's engine rumble to life.

Then they pulled off, speeding away into the desert.

She closed her eyes, feeling the wind on her face. It was like a dream. Sun on her skin and Smith's big body pressed up against hers.

After several days of hell, Kinsey finally felt safe.

Safer than she'd ever felt before.

SMITH NEGOTIATED the desert track carefully, Kinsey's slight weight pressed against his back. He didn't want to do anything to risk her coming off the bike. She'd been hurt enough.

The image of her swollen, bruised face ricocheted around his head. As he stared ahead, he felt equal parts pissed and relieved.

She was alive, but she was bruised to hell. A part of him wanted to go back and beat up those bastards some more.

Finally, the X8 came into view, and he watched a Black Hawk helicopter sweep overhead. As they got closer, he saw another, larger helicopter parked by the X8. This was a heavy-lift helicopter—a Sikorsky CH-53K *King Stallion*. He knew they'd use it to take the wreck of the X8 back to base.

The rest of the team was gathered around the King Stallion. Everyone was standing and clearly mobile, and he let out a breath. Looked like they were all okay. Several armed Air Force guards patrolled the wreck site. As Smith and Kinsey got closer, he saw guns swivel in their direction.

Lachlan strode forward, waving them down.

Smith pulled the bike to a stop in front of the group.

"Where the fuck did you go?" Lachlan's golden eyes were pissed.

"Couldn't let them get away and risk the chance of losing Kinsey again."

Lachlan stepped forward. "Kinsey." He cupped her cheek.

"I'm okay." Her voice was soft.

"Oh, God, Kinsey." Blair pushed forward and hugged her. Callie was right behind her, eyeing Kinsey's injuries carefully.

Kinsey smiled at Blair. "You're ruining your badass reputation by hugging me, you know."

Blair's nose wrinkled. "Screw it. If anyone doesn't think I'm badass, I'll kick their ass."

Axel bumped Blair out of the way to give Kinsey a quick kiss on the forehead, which made Smith scowl at him. The man was way too much of a charmer...best he kept his lips off Kinsey from now on.

"Callie?" Smith looked at the medic. "You need to check her over."

Callie moved in, holding her backpack. "Here." She eyed Kinsey again. "Well, they did a number on you, girlfriend." Callie lifted a penlight, shining it in Kinsey's eyes. "Any injuries I can't see?"

Kinsey gingerly shook her head. "I got a few hits to the stomach and ribs, but nothing hurts too bad. I do have a humdinger of a headache."

The calmly recited words made Smith want to kill someone.

"They were set up in a cabin off to the northwest,"

Smith said. "I left one dead in the desert, two of them tied up at the cabin—" he dragged in a breath "—and one got away. With the fake artifact."

Lachlan swiveled, barking orders to a group of guards. "I want those men brought in. Now!"

The guards jumped in a Humvee and took off.

"We'll question them," Lachlan said. "Find out who the hell they are."

"And show them that they messed with the wrong people." Axel's voice vibrated with anger.

Smith gave a short nod. "Didn't see anything to give any indication who they work for."

The Team 52 leader looked at Kinsey. "Kinsey? Did you hear anything? They say what they want?"

She hunched her shoulders. "No. They were careful never to use names around me. I heard them talking on the phone to others. There are more than just these four who kept me captive."

Lachlan nodded. "Okay. Let me check on the X8 recovery, then we'll get you back to base."

"I need to treat your cuts and bruises," Callie said.

Once again, Smith stared at Kinsey's battered face, anger churning in his gut. He noticed her turn to look at the twisted wreck of the X8, and her teeth sank into her bottom lip.

"You okay?" he asked.

A big, blue eye swung his way. "If only I hadn't fallen for their delivery con at the Bunker, and let them grab me—"

"Hey." He gripped her upper arms, interrupting her. "This isn't your fault."

Her eyes turned miserable. "I was stupid. I wasn't careful enough."

"Stop that," he growled.

Then, because he couldn't stop himself from touching her, he cupped her face. Again, the damage to her smooth skin made him so angry. Kinsey was always bright smiles and a pretty face. She had a hell of a smile that could blind any man or woman. She didn't deserve the bruises, cuts, and swelling. He stroked one bruise gently.

"We'll find out who they are," he said. "This is no one's fault but those mother...assholes. I'm sorry they ever laid a hand on you."

"Smith—"

"From now on, you'll be safe. I promise."

She nodded. "I know."

Minutes later, a Black Hawk helicopter swooped in to land. Smith kept Kinsey close as they boarded. Once all of Team 52 were seated, the helo took off.

Kinsey leaned into Smith's side. He slid an arm around her. Damned if she didn't fit perfectly against him. When he looked down, he realized that she'd fallen asleep. He knew she needed the rest.

Then he looked up.

Axel and Blair were grinning at him. Lachlan's lips were tipped in a smile, and Callie was studiously looking out the window, but she was smiling, too.

"Shut up," Smith muttered.

Blair leaned forward. "Dude, there is no way in hell we aren't going to get some mileage out of this."

He grunted. The team had roasted both Lachlan and

43

Seth when the men had fallen hard for their women on previous missions.

But this wasn't that. Kinsey was a part of the team, and theirs to protect. He was just looking out for her. Smith wasn't going there with her...ever.

He knew not everyone was better in pairs. He preferred his own company. When he'd been young and dumb, he'd let his high school girlfriend lead him around by his cock. He should never have let Lila convince him to get married. As soon as she had his ring on her finger, she'd gone about making his life a goddamn misery— spending his money, staying out all night, snorting shit up her nose, going off on drunken rants, and sometimes, she'd gotten violent.

Nope, Smith prized his solitude. Most relationships went south once the shine wore off, and he wasn't willing to go there again.

Blair leaned back in her seat, putting her arms behind her head. "The bigger they are—"

"The harder they hit annoying teammates," Smith finished.

Blair laughed, and he felt the amusement of the others, but when he looked back down at Kinsey, he couldn't dredge up much annoyance.

When they landed at Area 52, Kinsey didn't stir. Not wanting to disturb her, Smith lifted her into his arms.

She felt so tiny. She barely weighed a thing. When he leaped off the Blackhawk, she still didn't wake up. Instead, she snuggled deeper into his arms, trusting him to take care of her.

That was a trust Smith would do his best not to betray.

CHAPTER FIVE

K insey stepped out of the shower and looked at
herself in the mirror. She winced. It did not look
pretty. She had bruises everywhere, although the spectacular colors on her face were the worst of it.

She dried off and dressed quickly. She kept quarters
at Area 52 for the times she came out for training, or to
help on certain missions. She grabbed some cargo pants
and a long-sleeved T-shirt from the closet.

She felt cold, even after a long, hot shower. She
pulled her clothes on, breathing in the clean scent of
detergent and softener. You appreciated the small things,
after being held captive for days.

But she still couldn't seem to get warm.

Callie had worked hard, treating her injuries. The
medic had used some fancy machine that Ty had
invented, and done some sort of laser treatment on
Kinsey's bruising. She'd promised that it would increase
the rate of healing, and she'd see some fading within a

few hours. Callie had also given Kinsey some painkillers, so right now, she wasn't in any pain.

What she needed was to get back to work. To keep busy, and find out who the hell those bastards were who used her to threaten the team.

When she opened the door of her quarters, she halted. Smith was standing in the hallway, leaning against the wall.

When he spotted her, he straightened. "Feeling better?"

Suddenly, the impact of the last few days all crashed in on her. "No."

His gaze sharpened on her face. Without thinking, Kinsey made a beeline for him. She didn't care that he'd think she was weak or needy. She needed a hug.

She slammed into his chest. Gosh, he was so big and warm. So strong.

She started shaking, and his arms closed around her. "Hey, you're safe."

"I know, it's just..." Her throat tightened, cutting off her words.

Smith scooped her up in his arms. He strode into her room, kicked the door shut behind him, and sat down on her bunk. He pulled her into his lap.

Oh. How many times had she dreamed of being right here? She pressed into him. "You must think I'm weak—"

"You just suffered a traumatic kidnapping, Kinsey. You were beaten. Give yourself a break." One of his big hands stroked her back. "Take your time."

She had no idea how long they sat there, but slowly

the warmth of him seeped into her. She released a sigh. "I bet you've never been afraid."

"You'd be wrong. Been afraid loads of times. As a SEAL, in training, on missions."

She glanced up at him, wishing she could stroke that dark beard of his. "How did you cope?"

"I learned to channel it. Use it to help me get the job done. And after a rough mission, I learned not to bottle shit up. I learned to talk it out."

She gave a startled laugh. "You? Talk?"

He gave her the faintest smile. "I talk sometimes. With my team." He tucked her hair behind her ear, then fiddled with the strands for a moment, rubbing them between his fingers.

"Smith?"

"Your hair looks like spun gold."

Kinsey felt a flush of pleasure.

"You need to call your family?" he asked.

Her belly curdled. "No."

His fingers tightened on her. "No?"

"We're not close. Well, I am with my sister, but I'll call her when I get back to Las Vegas. She's working nights this week, so she wouldn't expect to hear from me until the weekend. She's a blackjack dealer at Caesar's Palace." Okay, maybe she was babbling a bit now.

Smith tilted his head, his gaze narrowed. "And your parents?"

"I haven't seen them for seven years. Not since I moved to Vegas." Not since she'd hightailed it out of Sugarview.

His brows drew together. "You came to Vegas alone?"

"Yes. I wanted to be a showgirl." She wrinkled her nose. "Then I found out I was two inches too short."

"Your parents let you move to Las Vegas alone?"

"They didn't have a choice. I was twenty by then." She'd finished high school and then spent two years working her butt off as a waitress and squirreling away every dollar she made into her Las Vegas Showgirl fund. "I couldn't wait to leave." She looked down at the floor. "Um, home wasn't...great."

"How was it not great?"

His tone had darkened and her heart thumped. "It doesn't matter. The past is the past." She smiled at him and watched his gaze drop to her lips. "Last thing my mama told me was that I wasn't smart enough to do anything important."

"Your mama sounds like a bitch."

Kinsey laughed. "Like you wouldn't believe."

A wave of tiredness hit her, and she dropped her head to his shoulder. She didn't want to let him go, but she knew she had to. The longer she snuggled into him the more she liked it.

"I felt afraid today," he said suddenly.

She blinked up at him.

"And yesterday. And the day you were taken."

Her lips parted. "You did?"

"When I knew they had you...I've never felt fear like that."

Kinsey's mouth dropped open and she stared at him. Her pulse was dancing like crazy.

Then, Smith leaned forward and pressed his mouth to hers.

The kiss was slow and gentle. *So good.*

As his lips moved over hers, his tongue sliding against hers, all kinds of sensations ignited inside Kinsey. She was kissing Smith. Oh God, she was kissing Smith and he was kissing her back. And it was better than she'd ever imagined.

She leaned closer, deepening the kiss. A small, husky sound broke free from her lips.

Then Smith jolted. He froze, stiller than she'd ever seen anyone go. Abruptly, he stood, dropping her onto her feet.

"I'm sorry, Kinsey. I should never have done that."

He looked horrified. *God.* Humiliation rushed over her. The man didn't want her. He'd made that clear before when, after one too many cocktails, she'd made a pass at him when the team was out one time.

"Sure. Just heat-of-the-moment relief, right?" She forced the words out of a parched throat.

He stared at her for a beat. "We'd better go and meet with the others."

An awkward silence fell. Well, that was that.

Fighting back the prick of tears, Kinsey hurried out of the room. She was excruciatingly aware of him striding beside her, but she couldn't look at him. She was suddenly cold again and she wrapped her arms around herself.

When they stepped into the computer room, she saw that everyone was there. Blair hurried over and bumped her shoulder against Kinsey's.

"You look better already. Your cheeks are flushed."

Kinsey managed a smile. "I'm feeling much better."

Computer genius extraordinaire Brooks came over, his slightly-too-long hair falling over his forehead, and his glasses framing dark-blue eyes. His shirt made her want to laugh. It said "the Force is strong with this one" with an arrow pointed upward.

Brooks patted her shoulder. "Shit, Kinse, you scared us."

"I'm okay."

"You find out who these assholes are yet?" Smith said.

Brooks turned, his face changing. He looked pissed. "No. I'm running all kinds of searches in conjunction with the levitation technology. Haven't found anything yet."

"That's what they wanted?" Kinsey asked.

Brooks nodded. "An ancient Tibetan levitation instrument."

Wow. It still amazed Kinsey every day that there were ancient artifacts with such power on Earth.

"What about the men from the cabin?" Smith looked at Lachlan. "You questioned them?"

Lachlan drew in a breath. "They were gone when the team arrived to retrieve them."

Smith cursed.

"Whoever they are, they're going to get a rude surprise when they realize the artifact they took doesn't work," Blair said.

"Do you think..." Kinsey cleared her throat. "Do you think once they know, they'll try to snatch me again?"

"Possibly," Brooks said. "We just don't know anything yet."

"We'll step up security," Smith promised. "They won't get near you again."

"Brooks is going to rig the Bunker with increased cameras and alarm systems," Lachlan added.

"And your place, too," Smith said.

"My place?" She frowned at him.

"Your apartment. Do you have an alarm system?"

She shook her head.

Smith crossed his arms over his chest. "I'll take a look at your security when we get back to Las Vegas. Ensure your place is secure."

Well, he might not want to kiss her, but she had no doubt he wanted to help keep her safe.

"Thanks."

SMITH PULLED the black SUV to a stop in front of the small block of apartments. He eyed the building, not liking what he was seeing. They were a step up from crappy...barely.

"I know it's not much," Kinsey said from the passenger seat. "But the rent is cheap, and it's close to the airport." She smiled. "Short commute."

Damn, the woman could find a silver lining in everything. He eyed the way her smile brightened her face. He was fucking glad the bruises on her face looked better—the treatment Callie had used had made them fade substantially—because every time he saw them, he wanted to punch someone.

"This was my first place when I moved to Las Vegas,"

she continued. "I never found any reason to move out, even once I could afford to. Besides, it's much better than where I grew up." She opened her door and slid out.

The more hints he got of Kinsey's past, the less he liked it. Smith got out of the SUV, and once she joined him, they walked up the crumbling path. The garden beds close to the building were full of overgrown plants. He also noted several lights were burned out. Place wasn't safe.

She led him up a set of external stairs to the second floor.

She stopped in front of her door and paused to stare at a vase filled with wilted red roses beside her door.

Smith scowled at the flowers. "What's that?"

"Um, nothing." She scooped up the flowers and pulled her keys out.

Two apartments down, a door swung open, and a middle-aged man wearing a ratty bathrobe popped his head out. "Hey, Kinsey."

Instantly, Smith didn't like the way the man looked at her.

"Hi, Roger." Kinsey's voice told Smith she didn't much like Roger either.

"Shit, what happened to your face?" Roger asked, morbid curiosity in his tone.

"Had an accident," Kinsey said, voice flat.

Roger lifted his chin. "Bummer." His gaze skimmed down her body. "Haven't seen you round much lately."

Kinsey opened her door. "I've been busy."

Smith stepped forward, and that's when Roger noticed him. The man automatically stepped back.

Roger puffed his chest up. "Uh...who's your friend?"

Kinsey tucked a strand of her hair back. "This is Smith, he's my—"

"Man," Smith finished, glaring at Roger. He ignored Kinsey's jerk of surprise.

Disappointment flashed on Roger's face. "Ah, right. Well, good night, then." Roger closed his door.

Kinsey stepped inside and Smith followed. She flicked on a light.

She spun to face him. "What was that all about?"

"I don't like him."

"That makes two of us. But he's an annoyance who stares at my chest. He's harmless."

Smith begged to differ. But instead of arguing, he turned his attention to her place. It was simple and worn. Small, open-plan living area and kitchen. She'd put her stamp on the place with splashes of color. Colored fabric in blues and pinks was draped over the curtains and over one lamp. There was a sagging couch, covered in a mound of brightly-colored pillows. Hell, it looked like the damn things were breeding.

There were also candles everywhere. Long ones, squat ones, thin ones, thick ones in glass jars. They were all different colors. He also spotted several more vases of roses crowded on her small kitchen counter. Who the hell was sending her all these flowers?

"Someone brought by bag back from the Bunker." She lifted the large handbag, pulling out her cellphone.

"Blair," Smith said.

Automatically, he strode over to the windows. He'd already noted the lock on her door was mediocre at best, but shit, the locks on her windows were crap. He noticed a postage-stamp-sized balcony outside. He scowled. They were one story up, so it'd be an easy climb.

He swiveled and strode down the short hall.

"Smith—"

He ignored her. There was a tired bathroom with garish green tiles, and a snug bedroom. He paused, staring at the bed. It had a pretty white cover, and another pile of out-of-control pillows, this time in soft pastels.

Feminine. Pretty.

"Smith?" She stood in the hall watching him, chewing on her bottom lip.

Looking at her lips only made him remember how good she tasted. Desire punched into his gut. She'd felt perfect in his arms, and she'd come alive for him, kissing him back hungrily.

Fuck. "Security is shit, babe."

"Okay."

"Tomorrow, I'll change the locks and install a security system."

Her eyes widened. "I don't think my landlord will—"

"Nothing to do with your landlord. I'll do it."

She blew out a breath, still chewing that lip. "Thanks."

Back in the living area, he stopped by her kitchen table. It was covered in old newspaper that she'd laid out and on top of that, it was filled with...stuff. He frowned, studying the tins, bags, empty pots, glass jars, rows of small bottles that contained oils, and stained utensils. He lifted his gaze.

She shrugged a shoulder. "I make candles in my spare time. I like them and they can get expensive, so I started making my own. They look nice and smell nice." Another shrug. "I never had pretty things growing up, so now I make sure I have lots of them."

A woman like Kinsey deserved pretty things.

"Who's sending the flowers?" he asked.

Her gaze skittered away.

"Babe?"

She looked back. "I don't know. Guess I have a secret admirer. They don't know me very well because I hate red roses."

Smith didn't like it. Not at all. "Tonight, I'm staying."

Her head shot up. "What?"

"I'm sleeping on the couch." No one was coming after her again.

He saw a flash of relief on her face. She'd been afraid to be alone, but in typical Kinsey fashion, she hadn't said a thing.

"I've got a bag and change of clothes in the SUV."

She nodded. "I don't know how to thank you for everything."

"No need to thank me, Kinsey."

She cocked a hip. "It's polite to say thank you, Smith." Her voice lowered. "You came for me, you helped me, and you're keeping me safe. No one's ever done that for me before." She smiled. "So, thank you."

Smith's hands curled into fists to keep from reaching for her. She couldn't be this sweet and nice. No one was. He remembered Lila had been all sugary sweetness... until his ring was on her finger. Then she'd been acid.

Lila hadn't been beautiful like Kinsey, but she'd been pretty easy on the eyes. He'd learned young that beauty could hide rot.

Kinsey nodded. "I'll get you a pillow and blanket."

He stared after her in confusion as she disappeared into her bedroom. But every instinct in Smith, everything he'd ever seen of Kinsey, told him she was the real deal. How could no one take care of a woman like Kinsey? She was everything that deserved to be protected.

Heading back into the living room, Smith kicked his boots off. He was running on fumes after days of little sleep. He needed some rest so he could stay alert.

How the hell he was going to sleep, knowing Kinsey was sprawled in that pretty bed only one room away, he had no idea.

He shoved some pillows off the couch and dropped down. He pulled out his SIG Sauer and set it on the coffee table. Then he gripped the back of his shirt and pulled it over his head.

"Here you—" Kinsey halted in the doorway. "Oh."

He looked up and saw her staring at his chest. It took all his willpower not to surge up and reach for her.

But he had reasons to stop that kiss back at the base. She'd had a terrible experience and she was vulnerable. He wasn't going to take advantage of that.

And on top of that, he had his own personal reasons to avoid relationships. He was a loner at heart, and he couldn't give Kinsey what she needed.

After a moment, she appeared to come unstuck. "There you go." She dropped the pillow and blanket on the couch. "Um, I'll..." She backed up. "I'm tired. I'll..."

"Night, Kinsey."

She nodded. "Good night, Smith." She turned and hurried down the hall.

Smith rose and slipped his boots back on. After a quick trip to the SUV to get his bag, he came back in, ensuring the locks were secured. He circled the room to check the locks before flicking off the lights. He looked out the window, scanning the parking lot and street. Nothing out of the ordinary.

Moving back to the couch, he dropped down and stretched out. It was too short for his long frame, but when he went hunting with his dad, they roughed it, and as a SEAL, he'd slept in some pretty awful conditions. This was plush by comparison.

He shoved the pillow under his head, and stared at the ceiling. He heard Kinsey moving around, and then her light clicked off.

Exhaustion tugged at him, and it wasn't long before Smith dozed off.

He woke to a whimper and a cry.

He knifed up, already reaching for his gun. He rushed into Kinsey's bedroom.

In the faint light coming through the window, he saw her sitting on the bed, sheets twisted around her body.

"Kinsey?"

She blinked. "Sorry. Bad dream. I don't even remember it." She pushed her hair back. Even in the shadows, his gaze went to the thick, sexy mass. "I'm sorry I woke you."

A cloud of tangled gold framed her face, which was softened by sleep. He liked her fresh-faced. Her skin glowed and didn't really need makeup. He thought she looked just as gorgeous without it.

She pushed the sheet back, and that's when he realized she was only wearing a tiny tank and even tinier shorts that left her slender legs bare. His cock twitched. *Hell.*

But he also saw she was shivering.

He frowned. The room wasn't cold. He tucked his SIG in the back of his jeans, and sat on the edge of her bed.

Smith reached for her and she was already moving. As he pulled her into his chest, she burrowed against him. He rested his cheek on the top of her head. She fit so well against him.

They sat there for a while before she pulled back.

"God. I keep plastering myself against you." In the faint light, he saw that her cheeks had gone pink. "You've made it clear you aren't...um...interested in me...so.... I'm sorry. I don't want you to feel awkward."

Smith stilled. "You think I'm not attracted to you?"

She looked away. "I've kissed you twice, and you pushed me away each time. I've gotten the message, so I don't want you to think I'm—"

Damn. He realized just how she'd taken him pushing her away. He'd been telling himself he was protecting them both from a mistake, but he'd been hurting Kinsey in the process.

He cupped her jaw and forced her gaze to his. "Look at me."

That gorgeous face turned up to his, confusion scrunching her brow.

"You've had a really bad few days."

She nodded.

"You've been hurt. You're vulnerable. I won't take advantage of that."

She nodded again, still looking confused.

Smith hauled her closer and the scent of her hair hit him. Strawberries. She smelled like strawberries. So damn sweet.

He tipped her face up and pressed his lips to hers. He kissed her. Deep, but slow, careful not to hurt her still-bruised face.

She made a sound, and just like before, she ignited. She shifted, straddling him and wrapping her arms around his neck.

Shit. As she deepened the kiss and ground her hips against his throbbing cock, he let out a groan. He bumped his hips, making sure she felt just how hard he was. His hardness against her softness.

She went still and her gaze met his.

"Think we can do away with the fucked-up notion that I don't want you?"

"But—"

"I'm a loner, Kinsey. I suck at relationships. I'm selfish, and prefer my own company."

Her face softened. "Smith—"

"No." He shook his head. "The fact that I'm attracted to you changes nothing. You deserve a man who can give you what you need."

Her gaze narrowed. "I get to say what I need, Smith."

"Kinsey—"

She shook her head. "No. I grew up with people

telling me I deserved nothing. And you are a good man. One of the best I know."

Fuck. Did she really think that? He twisted, pressing her onto the bed. He leaned over her and she undulated against him one more time. He gritted his teeth and cupped her cheek.

"I want you, Kinsey. But you and me...it's not going to happen."

She looked like he'd hit her, and it was an arrow to his gut.

"It's for the best," he said.

"Sure. Okay." She shoved at him and he rolled off her.

"I want us to be friends," he said.

She winced.

Shit. That sounded lame. "We're both tired, and you're healing, and your apartment isn't secure." He wanted to touch her, but she wrapped her arms around herself, not meeting his gaze. "Your security needs to be my priority right now."

"Okay, Smith." Her voice was flat.

"Now, get some sleep. I'm close by, and no one is getting to you. Understand?" He rose to his feet.

"Understood." Those big, blue eyes bored into him.

And because he was a selfish bastard and couldn't stop himself, he leaned down and rubbed his thumb over her lips. "Sweet dreams, sunshine."

CHAPTER SIX

Kinsey woke slowly, taking her time to shake off sleep. She snuggled into her pillow. It always took her forever to wake up in the morning, and fight off the grogginess. She envied people who leaped out of bed early, fresh as a daisy.

She always felt like a wilted blossom, left out in the hot sun and trodden on.

Blinking, she finally dragged herself out of her bed and stumbled toward the bathroom. She needed coffee. Sweet, sweet coffee.

She lifted her head and caught her reflection in the mirror. The sight of her face scared off a lot of the fog. *Eek.* The bruising was turning some interesting colors, but thankfully they were fading. She closed her eyes, fighting off the cascade of memories.

You're safe now, Kinsey. You aren't a prisoner.

Carefully, she washed her face, grabbed her cotton-candy-pink robe off the door—a gift from her sister—and headed out to the kitchen. Now, she really needed coffee. A gallon of it.

When she reached the end of the hall, she spied the long, jeans-clad legs stretched out on the couch. Kinsey froze.

She took another two steps.

Smith, wearing only jeans that she could see were undone, was still asleep. He wasn't wearing a shirt. *He wasn't wearing a shirt.* She pulled in a short breath. He was so ripped, that body all strength and power. He had a wide chest, huge, muscular arms, and God, so many abs. There was an intriguing smattering of hair across his chest. She let her gaze run down his long legs—like she could stop herself—all the way to his bare feet.

She sucked in a breath. One of his feet was made of metal. She blinked. She hadn't known that Smith had a prosthetic. He'd never let on. He always moved with power and an athletic grace she admired. Looking at the sleek lines of the prosthetic, she knew it had to be one of Ty's creations. Her gaze switched to Smith's other foot. She'd never thought much about feet before, but his were long and well-shaped, and somehow it felt incredibly intimate to be looking at his feet—both flesh and metal.

He was so breathtaking. And he was attracted to *her.* Her heart hit against her ribs. And he'd said that they were never going to happen.

The pain hit her again. He couldn't want her anywhere near as much as she wanted him. Or he'd take a chance on them. Kinsey would climb mountains or fight wars for a chance to be with Smith.

And he wanted to be *friends.*

She remembered every second of that moment on her bed. His mouth on hers. A glimpse at everything she wanted, only to have him pull it away again. Just like everything else she'd ever wanted in life.

Coffee. She really needed coffee.

Stumbling into the kitchen, she set to work. She'd just filled her coffee machine with water, when she heard a deep rumble.

"You're awake."

She glanced over her shoulder and watched him stalk into the small kitchen, somehow filling it completely with his presence. She blinked a few times.

"Kinsey?"

"Yeah?"

His lips quirked, and he rubbed a hand against his chest. "Sleep well?"

There was so much bare chest and she couldn't look away. She wanted to touch him.

"Kinsey?"

"Um, yeah. I did. Sleep well."

He smiled now, and the sight of it blinded her.

"Never would have picked you for a morning zombie," he said.

She scowled. "I need coffee." *And I want you so badly it hurts.*

"Is it ready?"

She shook her head and opened the cupboard. She reached for the packet of coffee beans, only to have it crumple in her hands.

Empty.

All that was left was an empty packet.

Dammit. "I'm out of coffee beans." She swiveled. "There's a great little coffee place just around the corner. They make a mean latte." She eyed him. He probably drank his coffee black and thick, like tar.

Smith lifted his chin. "Get dressed." His gaze skimmed over her face before drifting down her body.

Suddenly, Kinsey felt hot. She quickly pushed past him and escaped the kitchen. She took a few minutes to brush her teeth, then tame her hair, and dab on some makeup in the incredibly vain hope of hiding the bruises. She snorted. Yeah, and she might win the jackpot next time she stuck a coin in a slot machine.

Oh, well. She set her shoulders back. She was alive, and that was what was important.

Next, she slipped into her favorite jeans, and pulled on a long-sleeved, Caesars Palace T-shirt her sister had given her.

She was heading out to meet Smith when her phone rang. She snatched it up and saw it was her sister. "Hey, sis."

"Did you fall off the face of the Earth, K? I left you a bunch of messages."

Kinsey tucked the phone between her shoulder and ear, and slipped her shoes on. "Well, kind of." In the briefest of terms, she relayed the story of her abduction.

There was silence.

"Kitty?"

"What the fuck!" Kitty exploded.

Kinsey held the phone away from her ear.

"You were kidnapped?" her sister screeched.

"I'm fine. I'm home. I'm one-hundred-percent okay."

"You've always been damn cagey about that job of yours." Kitty huffed out a breath. "You said it wasn't dangerous."

"I said it isn't usually dangerous. Look, everything's fine, I promise. My...workmates came to get me." She saw movement and looked up to see Smith in the doorway, watching her. He'd pulled a flannel shirt on.

"I'm coming over," Kitty said.

"No."

"You shouldn't be alone."

"You just got off night shift, K, and you go on shift again tonight. You need some sleep." Her sister had recently bought a sweet condo not too far from The Strip. She had a mortgage to pay. "And...I'm not alone."

There was another pause. "Who's there?"

She stared at Smith's big form. "A friend from work."

"A female friend or a male friend?"

"What's that matter?" Kinsey said.

"Why does your voice sound funny?"

"It does not."

Smith moved closer, the heat of him washing over her. He lifted a hand, one finger moving over the bruises on her cheek. Her breath hitched.

"Smith." His name came out without her meaning it.

"Smith?" Kitty pounced. "That's his name. What's he look like?"

His fingers drifted up, rubbing her hair between his fingers.

"Kitty, we're heading out for coffee. I'm okay. I'll call you soon, I promise."

Her sister sighed. "You always have to be so independent, don't you? Okay. I love you, K."

"I love you, too, K. Bye." Kinsey ended the call. "My sister."

"I got that. You two are close?"

"Yeah. We can fight, but it's always been the two of us against the world." Kinsey grabbed the keys off her hall table and they headed out the door.

As they walked out onto the sidewalk, she watched Smith scan their surroundings. When they reached the street, he nudged her away from the street side of the sidewalk, placing himself between her and the road.

Her heart did a little flip-flop. He was taking care of her. Again.

He slung an arm across her shoulders. *Oh.* That felt nice. His body brushed against hers.

"Do you have siblings?" she asked.

"No. Only child. My parents divorced when I was young, they can't stand each other."

"Oh. Sorry."

"They're better when they're apart. I split my time between both of them."

Kinsey nodded. He'd been lucky to have parents who wanted to spend time with him.

She tipped her face up. The sun was shining and she pulled in a deep breath. She smiled. It felt so good to feel the air on her face, and the sun on her skin.

She realized Smith was staring at her again, his gaze locked on her lips.

"What?" she asked.

"You seem to find pleasure in everything. Even the small things. Especially the small things."

Growing up in a dirty trailer with a drunken dad and an angry mom, she'd had to find happiness in the small things.

"Life's too short not to," she said.

"Yeah."

They reached the coffee shop. The tables outside were crowded, and as they moved inside the small space, Kinsey walked toward the counter, smiling. She ordered a skinny caramel latte and, as she suspected, Smith got a black Americano.

He paid and they waited for their drinks.

Kinsey spotted a stack of newspapers, and reached out to flick through one. She didn't often read or watch the news. She found it so depressing.

She sensed someone move closer to them and glanced up. A tall, fit woman in tight leggings and a cropped sports top—that showed off a set of tight abs—was eyeing Smith like he was water, and she'd been lost in the desert for days.

Kinsey's belly clenched. She'd never seen Smith with a woman, but she'd heard Blair and Callie talk before. When Smith hooked up, it was with tall, built women.

Kinsey knew she wasn't short, but she wasn't ripped and athletic, either.

"Latte and Americano for Smith," the barista called out. Smith grabbed the drinks, and when he turned, the woman made her move.

"Hey, there." The woman grabbed his bicep.

He frowned and looked down at her.

Gah. Kinsey had no desire to watch this. The woman acted as if Kinsey wasn't even there. She reached out and grabbed her drink out of Smith's hand. Before he could say anything, she spun and headed for the door.

Turning her back on them, Kinsey headed outside and onto the sidewalk. She sipped her latte, and for the first time in a long time, even her first sip of coffee didn't taste that good.

A man bumped into her and she lost her grip on the drink. It flew out of her hand, and hit the concrete, spilling everywhere.

"Hey," she complained, looking up.

She stared into a hard face. He had olive skin, dark, curly hair and eyes so dark they looked black. He wrapped a hand around her arm and started dragging her down the sidewalk.

Fear spurted to life inside her. "Let me go." This *wasn't* happening again.

"Shut up and you won't get hurt."

Screw this. Kinsey dropped her weight. It sent the guy off balance, and he cursed in what sounded like Italian as they staggered.

Her attacker grabbed for her again, but she dodged. She kicked at him, aiming for between his legs. But he twisted at the last minute and her foot hit his thigh.

He growled, gripped her waist, and tossed her over his shoulder.

"Let me go, asshole!" She twisted violently, trying to break free.

Suddenly, there was a screech of tires and a white van pulled up at the curb.

She sucked in a breath. *Oh, no.*

Kinsey kept squirming, desperate to break free. *Where the hell was Smith?*

ANNOYED with the woman who'd stopped him so she could flutter her eyelashes at him, Smith stomped out the door of the coffee shop.

He was also pissed that Kinsey had headed out without waiting for him. As he opened the door, he heard the screech of tires and Kinsey's scream.

Smith dropped his coffee and charged.

In an instant, he saw some asshole had her over his shoulder, and she was fighting him.

Smith didn't make a sound. He shoved through some people, leaped over a chair, and ran. He saw the side door of the van at the curb slide open.

Hell, no.

He reached the guy carrying Kinsey and punched him hard in the kidneys.

The man shouted and dropped her. Smith caught her and yanked her close.

"Stay back." He shoved her behind him.

The guy spun, dark eyes widening as he took in Smith's form.

Smith slammed out with another punch, this time catching the man in the gut. He groaned, trying to swing his own fists.

Smith caught one hand, spun the guy, and shoved his arm up behind his back. And he didn't do it gently.

With a choked noise, the man went up on his toes, trying to ease the pain.

"Let him go."

Smith turned his head to look at the man who stepped out of the van. He was aiming a Glock directly at Smith.

Turning, Smith kept the man he held in front of him like a shield, reached back, and pulled his SIG from the small of his back.

He didn't bother with a warning. He kicked the knees out from under the guy in front of him. As soon as the man dropped to the ground, Smith aimed and fired on the second man.

With a cry, the man jerked, his gun hitting the ground. He clutched his bleeding arm, smacking into the side of the van.

"Kinsey, get the weapon," Smith ordered.

She darted forward and snatched it up. She lifted it, aiming at the bleeding man.

Smith strode forward, yanked open the passenger door of the van. He reached in and dragged a struggling man out.

One quick look assured him the van was empty. There were only three of the fuckers.

Smith dropped the man to the ground beside the first attacker. When he quickly leaped back up, Smith elbowed him in the throat. The man staggered, grasping his neck, and collapsed, gagging.

Smith yanked zip ties out of his pockets, and quickly started tying the three idiots up.

"Try to escape," Smith growled. "I want an excuse to

hit you again." He tied up the final one, dragging them into a line on the sidewalk.

When he looked up, Kinsey was looking at him, wide-eyed. The café's crowd was also silent, watching the scene in front of them with shocked expressions.

"Kinsey, call Brooks. Need some of the team here."

She nodded and pulled out her phone.

Smith reached into the van, and snatched the keys out of the ignition. He took the handgun from Kinsey.

"Blair and Axel are close," Kinsey said. "They're on their way."

Smith cupped her cheek. "You all right?"

She nodded.

He leaned down and brushed his mouth over hers. Her hands gripped his shirt.

His chest was tight. She could've been nabbed. Again. Anger surged and he tried to keep a hold on it.

He pulled her up on her toes. "You stay beside me. You don't walk outside without me."

"Smith—"

"Just nod and tell me you understand."

She huffed out a breath. "I understand."

Smith turned to the trussed-up, would-be kidnappers. Were these the same guys, or were they now dealing with someone else?

"Who do you work for?" he demanded.

All he got in reply were sullen looks and silence.

Smith took a menacing step closer and watched the men tense. Then he heard the roar of an engine. A red Mustang pulled to a halt behind the van. Blair and Axel leaped out.

"What the fuck?" Blair frowned at the men.

"They tried to snatch Kinsey." Smith heard the fury vibrating in his voice. He looked back at the men. "Who do you work for?"

Still no answer.

He took another step closer, and all of them looked uncomfortable. Smith squatted. "Keep it up. I know plenty of interesting ways to get you to talk."

"Bruno," the youngest man blurted out.

The name meant nothing to Smith. He looked at Blair and Axel, and they both shook their heads.

Blair pulled out her phone. "Brooks? Yeah, we got here. Got a name for you to run."

Axel stood nearby, hands on his lean hips. "What do you fuckers want?"

"We heard other interested parties were after the woman. That they'd nabbed her before, and there was something big involved." He licked his lips. "A powerful weapon."

Fuck. Smith gritted his teeth. These weren't even the same guys who'd taken Kinsey the first time.

Two more cars screeched to a stop beside them. Smith spotted a police cruiser and a Crown Victoria.

Blair stiffened. "Hell."

A tall man unfolded from inside the Crown Vic. He had thick, brown hair that curled at the collar of his dark shirt, and worn jeans. There was a badge clipped to his belt.

"Blair, always a pleasure." The man's long legs ate up the distance between them.

Blair crossed her arms over her chest, and glared. "I can't say the same, Detective MacKade."

"You beat these guys up?" MacKade asked her.

Blair's gaze narrowed. "No."

"Sure? I know you have a thing for slamming assholes into the ground."

"You keep prodding me, MacKade, and I'll show you how I beat an asshole up."

Axel made a choked sound, and wrapped an arm around her neck. He yanked her back.

"Nice to see you, Detective," Axel said.

MacKade stared at the arm Axel had around Blair for a beat, before turning to Smith. "Got a call that you guys needed some assistance."

Smith pulled Kinsey close. "These fuckers tried to grab Kinsey off the sidewalk and throw her in the van."

Luke MacKade's gaze took in Kinsey's battered face and his jaw tightened. "You're okay, darlin'?"

She nodded. "Smith stopped them."

"I'm surprised there isn't more blood." MacKade waved a hand at the uniformed officers. "Take them in." His gaze fell on the men, glittering. "We'll be charging you with assault and attempted abduction."

The men all stared at the ground. The uniforms yanked them up, and shoved them toward the cruiser.

Blair moved. "Come after her again, I'll yank your balls off and make you eat them."

The youngest man blanched, and even the cops eyed her warily.

MacKade laughed and shook his head. "Blood-thirsty." Then he leaned closer. "But don't make me arrest you. I already tidy up the messes you guys leave around Las Vegas."

Blair stiffened. "We have an important job to do."

"You could stay within the lines when you do it."

She hissed and leaned closer. "We save lives."

"So do I. Stay out of trouble, Blair." He nodded at Smith, Kinsey, and Axel, and then strode back to his vehicle.

Blair looked like steam was about to come from her ears. "That arrogant... Like I want to fight criminals and terrorists for fun."

"Cool it," Smith said.

Blair dragged in a breath, and when her gaze fell on Kinsey, she managed to rein in her temper. "You guys had breakfast?"

Kinsey shook her head. "And I only got one sip of my latte."

Blair nudged Smith aside, and slid an arm over Kinsey's shoulders. "Well, let's hit Griffin's for some bacon and eggs."

When Kinsey smiled, Smith felt something tight inside him loosen. She looked fine after the scuffle, sunshine beaming from her face. Resilient as fuck, and completely irresistible.

CHAPTER SEVEN

K insey was sitting on a stool at Griffin's Sports Bar and Grill, wedged in between two sets of broad shoulders. Smith was to her right, and Lachlan to her left.

The rest of Team 52 had met them at the bar, including Seth and his new wife January. They'd heard what had happened to Kinsey, and had cut their Tahitian honeymoon a few days short. She'd been hugged by everyone, and Seth had taken one look at her face and looked really angry.

The handsome, former CIA operative had glared at Lachlan, who looked equally as angry. "You should have fucking told me."

Lachlan lifted his chin. "She's okay."

Thankfully, Blair had sauntered up to the bar to order food and broken the tension. Now they were all seated at the bar, the conversation alternating between the latest football game and speculation on who the hell was behind the attack on Kinsey and the team. She leaned forward, stealing a glance down the bar. On the other side of Lachlan sat his woman, Rowan.

Rowan said something, her dark-red hair gleaming in the light, and leaned into Lachlan. And the scary, intense Lachlan smiled down at her. *Smiled.*

Kinsey sighed. The pair were so in love. The same applied to Seth and January, who just about glowed with happiness. Seth had an arm around his pregnant wife, looking pretty damn pleased with himself.

Smith shifted on his stool, his hard thigh brushing hers. Every single thought rushed out of her head.

Lachlan's phone rang.

The Team 52 leader lifted it to his ear. "Brooks, talk to me." A pause. "Uh-huh. Okay. Thanks." He ended the call and glanced at them all, waiting until the bartender moved away. "Guys MacKade took in are low level. They work for Sam Bruno. Small-time guy here in Las Vegas, with links to the Mafia. Claims he's descended from one of Bugsy Siegel and Mickey Cohen's lieutenants from Vegas' Mafia heyday in the 30s and 40s. They're into drugs, brothels, loans sharking, insurance fraud. They heard something was going down, got wind of Kinsey's name, and thought they'd wade in." Lachlan's flat, gold gaze met Kinsey's. "We'll make sure their interest in you ends now. MacKade's already paid their boss a visit, and he's a man who prefers to not be on the LVMPD's radar."

"Any news on the original assholes?" Smith asked.

"Nothing. Brooks can't pin them down. There were whispers about some sort of terrorist group, home grown, looking to branch out in bigger ways. But we've got nothing but rumors."

"Whoever they are," Smith said, "they're pretty ambitious, attacking us and going after the artifact."

Lachlan nodded. "We all know fanatics will risk anything for their cause, and the power-hungry are pretty damn driven."

Kinsey's belly curdled and she set her fork down. "Whoever they are, they'll know the artifact they have is fake by now."

"You're safe." Smith's big hand engulfed hers. His other one moved to the back of her neck.

As she looked into his eyes, she believed him. She knew he'd help keep her safe.

Soon, the conversation drifted to Seth and January's trip to Tahiti, with some good-natured ribbing about sand in uncomfortable places.

Smith pulled his phone out and she listened to him organizing for a new security system for her apartment, new locks for her doors and windows, and maintenance to some exterior lights. By the time he was finished, her place would be Fort Knox.

She sat there sipping her coffee as the others talked. Then she slid off her stool to head to the restroom. Smith grabbed her arm.

"Going to the ladies', big guy," she said.

He looked over her head, and then Blair and Callie rose as well. Kinsey screwed up her nose. She couldn't even go to the restroom alone.

In the somewhat dingy restroom, she did her thing and when she came out of the stall to wash her hands, Blair and Callie were watching her.

"So?" Callie said.

Kinsey lifted her head and caught Callie's gaze in the mirror. The brunette was grinning.

Blair was nearby, leaning against the wall with her arms crossed over her chest. She had a smile on her face.

"Smith is being very...protective," Callie said.

Blair snorted. "Overprotective. That man is in protection overdrive."

Butterflies took flight in Kinsey's belly. "That's just what he's like. He'd do the same for any one of us."

"No," Callie said. "I mean, he'd help keep us safe, but he wouldn't go all growly and defending-mountain-man."

"That man wants to drag you to his cabin and—" Blair grinned "—probably tie you to his bed. He likes you, Kinse."

"And I really like him." The confession came out of her in a rush. "But I've made that clear before, and he's pushed me away. He wants to be friends."

Both women grimaced.

"The idiot," Blair muttered.

"I think he just feels the need to protect me."

Blair shook her head. "He's not really the kind of guy to talk about his feelings, but he's been through a lot of tough stuff. He was a damn good SEAL, then he lost his foot on a mission."

"I didn't know," Kinsey said.

Blair lifted her chin. "I know he had a terrible year between the SEALs and Team 52 recruiting him. Surgery, therapy, drinking too much." Blair's bi-colored gaze zeroed in on her. "That bother you?"

Kinsey frowned. "What?"

"His foot."

79

Her frown deepened. "Why would it bother me?"

Blair relaxed, then shrugged a shoulder. "Some people might see it as a flaw."

"That's crazy. He's the most gorgeous man I've ever seen."

The two women grinned at her.

Then Callie's face turned serious. "And then there was his wife."

Kinsey jolted. "Wife?" Smith was *married*? She felt like she was going to hyperventilate.

"Ex-wife, now. He got hitched straight out of high school. By the sounds of things, she was a real bitch. Was honey-sweet at first, then she changed, spent his money like crazy, had a drug problem. He tried to help her, but she just wanted to party. He finally divorced her ass and joined the Navy."

God. Kinsey tried to take it in. What kind of woman would Smith marry? More importantly, what stupid woman would let a man like him slip away? Was she the reason he preferred being alone?

"Look, whatever's going on, right now, we have to focus on finding these bad guys." Kinsey knew they were all still in danger. Whether Smith was into her or not wasn't important.

"Don't you worry about the bad guys." Blair patted Kinsey's back. "We're going to sort this out and we'll keep you safe."

Callie winked. "Especially Smith."

Kinsey sighed, and together, the three of them headed back to the bar. She saw that the rest of the team had finished and were standing near the door.

Smith stepped forward. "Ready?"

She nodded. "We heading back to my apartment?"

"No." A muscle ticked in his jaw. "I've decided that you're moving in with me."

She heard all the team go silent. Kinsey blinked. "What?"

"Until we know for sure that you're safe, you stay at my place."

Behind her, she heard Blair and Callie start to laugh.

SMITH DROVE the SUV out of Vegas, Kinsey quiet beside him in the passenger seat. They were headed west, toward the Spring Mountains.

They'd stopped at her apartment, and she'd packed some clothes and things she needed. They left the city behind, and traded it for open space.

She frowned out the window. "Where do you live?"

"Have a cabin out here."

She smiled. "I couldn't picture you living in a condo, with neighbors. This makes much more sense."

But Smith saw the smile dissolve, and the worry was back in her eyes again.

"Hey." He reached over and gripped her knee. "You're safe."

She nodded. "I know." But the shadows in her eyes didn't lessen.

"You trust me?"

She glanced at him. "Yes."

"*No one* is getting to you."

"Okay."

He squeezed her knee, and then turned off the main road.

"Are you in the mountains?" she asked.

"No. At the base of them." His place was close enough for him to enjoy the view of the mountains, but cut his commute into the city.

They stopped at a gate. Smith climbed out to open it, drive them through, then closed it. They drove up the dusty desert road. The scraggly desert vegetation gave way to some hardy trees around his cabin. He finally pulled to a stop.

As he cut the engine, he worried what she'd think of it. His place wasn't fancy, and there was nothing for miles around. He liked his solitude.

They got out of the SUV and he saw her gaze on the place. He looked at the cabin, trying to picture it through her eyes. It was made of stone and wood, and definitely wasn't huge.

She glanced his way and smiled. "It's gorgeous, Smith."

He smiled back, his shoulders easing. Suddenly, a big dog bounded around the cabin, aiming straight at them.

The Great Dane paused, skidding in the dirt. It looked at Smith, then looked at Kinsey, then the hound made his choice. He bounded at Kinsey, jumped, and almost knocked her down.

"Hercules, down." Smith grabbed at his dog's collar.

"Who's this?" A huge smile broke out on Kinsey's face. She rubbed the dog's head. "Hello, handsome."

"This is Hercules. Who has no manners."

She rubbed down the canine's blue-gray-colored body, sending him into fits of delight. He let out a happy woof.

"Who takes care of him when you're gone?" she asked.

"Neighbor a few miles down the road. He comes up and feeds him." Smith patted Hercules' glossy coat.

Then he grabbed Kinsey's bag, and led her up the steps to his front door.

When they stepped inside, she looked around with interest. The living area was a simple room with stone floors, a small kitchen with butcher-block counter tops, and a big, stone fireplace that he loved.

He kept the place pretty tidy, but there wasn't much in the way of decoration. Not like the touches she had at her apartment.

He pointed toward the three doors off to one side. "Bedroom, bathroom, utility room. And that's about it."

"It's great, Smith. It has rustic charm." She poked her head into the utility room, pausing to stare.

The room was really more of a storage area. One wall was covered in gear—hiking gear, ropes, coats. The other wall was all glass-fronted cabinets. They were filled with his weapon collection—rifles, handguns, shotguns, knives.

"Um." She looked back over her shoulder. "Sure you have enough?"

He heard the teasing note in her voice. "You make candles, I collect weapons."

"Why don't you have them on display in the living area?"

He frowned. "I don't collect them as art pieces."

She coughed. "Right."

"I also have an excellent security system, including motion sensors around the boundaries of my property."

Her eyes widened. "Isn't that overkill?"

"No."

He dropped her bag in the bedroom. He had a simple, wooden bed with a dark-blue cover, and a blanket folded at the end with a desert motif.

He turned and saw Kinsey touching the rock over the fireplace. She was in his place.

He'd imagined her here before.

"I'm going to do the rounds outside." Hercules woofed, knowing what that meant. "Grab yourself a drink. Rest."

She nodded.

Smith slipped outside and walked around his property, Hercules bounding beside him. He first checked the shed where his Harley was stored. Everything was undisturbed and in its proper place. He scanned the horizon. He had actually understated his security system to Kinsey.

No one could get within a few miles of the cabin without him knowing. If anyone set off a sensor, he'd get an alert sent to his phone.

When Smith stepped back into the cabin, it was silent. Hercules headed to the kitchen and his water bowl. Smith froze. Where was Kinsey? He took two huge strides inside and then halted.

That's when he spotted her on the couch. Asleep.

His chest contracted. She wasn't here for him to take advantage of, or indulge his own fantasies. But damn, he liked seeing her in his space, her body tucked up on his cushions.

In his head, memories of the morning's kidnap attempt hit him hard. No fuckers were going to take her. He carefully sat beside her on the couch.

Her eyelids fluttered open. "Smith?"

He reached out and stroked her jaw. She reached back, returning the gesture, her fingers brushing along his beard. He slid a hand into her hair, clenching on the thick, shiny locks.

"Damn, I love your hair," he murmured.

She rose up, her gaze on his, and kissed him.

It started off gentle, a sweet exploration. But then it ignited. She made a hungry sound, and need roared through Smith. Fuck, he'd never tasted anything as good as Kinsey. He groaned.

She wrapped an arm around his neck and pressed into him.

He shifted. He couldn't take advantage. "Kinsey—"

But her hands gripped his shirt. "Don't pull back, Smith. *Please.*"

He groaned again and wrapped his arms around her. He couldn't deny her. He wouldn't make sweet, pretty Kinsey beg for what she wanted. He deepened the kiss, taking his time, never wanting to stop. Fuck it all. It was time to stop denying the one thing he wanted most of all.

He pressed her back onto the couch, and her hands slid under his shirt.

She let out a husky cry. "I love your body," she whispered. "You're so beautiful."

No one had ever called Smith beautiful before. She was the beautiful one.

"You're the beauty, babe. Inside and out." He lifted her shirt, his gaze taking in a pretty pink bra. *Damn.* He lowered his head, kissing her skin, trailing his lips over her. Then, he found one lace-covered nipple and sucked it into his mouth.

She writhed beneath him. "Smith—"

"Shh, baby, lie back. Enjoy." This was for her. All for her.

Her face was still bruised, and her body still battered, and he wanted to take care of her.

He reached for her jeans, slowly peeling them down her hips and legs. She sucked in a breath.

"This is all for you, sunshine." Smith slid his hand between her slim thighs, cupping her over the tiny lace panties. It was all for her, but there was no denying that he'd love every second of pleasuring her.

CHAPTER EIGHT

O*h, God.*
      Sensations crashed through Kinsey.

Smith—big, sexy Smith—was crouched over her, hands sliding along her body. He slid her panties down, and his mouth moved behind her knee. And then it traveled up her leg.

Oh. *Oh.* "Smith."

Then his mouth was between her thighs. She reached down and gripped his hair, her back arching off the cushion.

"Babe, you taste so good." He took his time lapping at her and she moaned. When he groaned against her, the sound vibrated through her, adding to her pleasure.

"Smith...I'm..." Her orgasm was looming closer. It'd never been this easy for her to come before. She could never seem to relax enough, and her partners were always in a rush.

"Let go, Kinsey. Come for me."

His hands cupped her bottom, lifting her up to his hungry mouth. Watching him pleasure her turned her on more.

"Smith!" She came in a huge rush. Her vision wavered.

Kinsey collapsed back on the couch, and when she could finally pry her eyes open, Smith's face was pressed to her belly.

"Gorgeous," he murmured.

She blushed. Then she took note of the hardness pressing against her leg. "Um, I really want you inside me."

His gaze glittered, then he turned his head, his beard scratching her skin as he pressed a kiss to her belly.

"This is for you," he said.

"But—"

He shifted up, cupping her cheek. Then he leaned down and kissed her. She tasted herself on his lips and her chest hitched. It was intimate and sexy.

"Just relax," he said.

She sank back against the cushions. "Okay."

He helped her pull her panties back on. Kinsey thought she should feel embarrassed, but she felt too good to really care.

Suddenly, a strange alarm began to sound from some-where nearby. Smith sat up fast, his body tensing. Hercules let out a loud woof. Smith grabbed his phone.

"What is that?" she asked.

"Sensor alarm."

"Really?" Kinsey's heart leaped into her throat.

Then he relaxed. "It's the guys."

With a squeak, Kinsey shoved him away. "I need to get dressed."

He smiled. "You look cute."

She glared at him and hurried to the bathroom.

When she returned, clothes straightened and hair brushed, a black SUV had pulled up out front. Kinsey watched Blair, Axel, and Callie emerge. Hercules bounded up to them.

"Pizza." Blair lifted the stack of pizza boxes she was carrying.

A gorgeous, restored sports car growled up the drive, pulling in behind the SUV. Seth and January slid out.

"Hi, Kinsey." The archeologist waved, but then her face turned white.

"Hellcat?" Seth asked, frowning.

Another wave. "I smelled the pizza. Just some queasiness."

Next, Kinsey heard the throb of a motorcycle engine. A sleek, hot bike rolled up and pulled to a stop in front of them. The rider set long legs down, while the smaller passenger sat tucked into his back. Kinsey saw the red strands of hair escaping the bike helmet and knew it was Rowan and Lachlan.

Rowan pulled her helmet off, looking flushed. *Hmm.* Kinsey studied the bike. She wondered how good it would feel to be tucked up behind Smith, cruising an empty highway somewhere. Yes, she'd ridden with him on that dirt bike in the desert, but it hadn't exactly been leisurely or relaxing.

Blair walked past Kinsey and into the cabin. She

paused, looked at Kinsey's face, then at Smith, and grinned.

God. Heat flared in Kinsey's cheeks. Could everyone tell that she and Smith had been fooling around?

Soon, they were all settled inside, draped over the couches, sitting backwards on chairs, or sprawled on the floor, eating pizza and drinking beer.

"Any updates from Brooks?" Smith asked.

"He sent through files on several potential terrorist groups." Lachlan set his beer down and grabbed his backpack. He pulled out several folders, dropping them on the coffee table. "I was going to wait until we finished eating, but everyone might as well start reading."

As they drank and ate, they flipped through the pages. Studying the different criminal groups made Kinsey feel a bit sick. Why would people do things like this? Hurt other people?

She listened to the team discuss the pros and cons of the different terrorist groups, and who might be a match for the men who'd taken Kinsey.

Despite the topic, she enjoyed the comraderie between them. She'd been out with them all before, but she'd never felt like part of this inner circle.

She went to get herself a drink from the kitchen and when she returned, Smith shifted his legs. She sat down on the floor in front of him and he pulled her closer. She pressed against his strong legs. Once again, she felt safe. Protected.

"Nothing is gelling." Smith dropped a file on the table with a grunt.

"This group has links to the Mafia." Rowan held up

her file. "They're rumored to have gone after artifacts before."

Smith straightened. "Heard some of the attackers in the desert talking. Heard a name mentioned. Enzo. That's Italian right?"

The pizza curdled in Kinsey's belly. "Enzo?"

Smith frowned at her, his gaze sharpening. "Ring a bell?"

"It's not really a common name, is it?" She set her beer down. "There was a guy I dated a few weeks back..." She swallowed. "His name was Enzo."

She heard a chorus of muttered curses.

"Full name?" Lachlan asked.

"Enzo Rossi." She shot to her feet. "He was pushy, clingy, and after a few dates I told him I didn't want to see him anymore. He wouldn't take no for an answer and sent me loads of flowers, boxes of chocolates." She grimaced.

"Those flowers at your place," Smith said. "They were from him?"

She nodded. "I've been giving them to a hospice near my place. I never told him about my work. *Never.*" She spun to face them. "I swear. He knew I worked at the airport, that was it."

God, this was all her fault. She'd been silly enough to be used. She remembered meeting Enzo. He'd "bumped" into her on the sidewalk and almost knocked her over. They'd laughed. He'd been good-looking, and she'd been feeling sorry for herself after Smith's rejection.

"I never told him anything—"

All of a sudden, hands gripped her hips and she was yanked into Smith's lap. "Babe. Chill."

She went still, her gaze caught by his eyes.

"We know you'd never talk. If he did learn things about you, he probably followed you to the Bunker, surveilled you."

She swallowed, hating the idea of Enzo watching her.

"Here." Blair set a tablet up on the coffee table. Brooks' face appeared on the screen.

Kinsey couldn't quite see the man's shirt, but it looked like the top of a stormtrooper's helmet on it.

"Guys, I ran Enzo Rossi. He has links to the Mafia."

"Shit," Blair uttered.

"Oh, God." Kinsey pressed a hand to her jumping belly.

Smith pressed a hand to the back of her neck. "This is good. We have a lead. This isn't your fault."

"Brooks, keep digging," Lachlan said. "I want to know everything about this guy. Who he hangs with, where he's based, who he works for, and what he damn well ate for breakfast." Lachlan stood. "Time to go. I want everyone rested up and ready to move as soon as we have something."

"Can I go back to work at the Bunker?" Kinsey asked. She wanted to work. She wanted to help.

Smith frowned. "No."

"Or at least not alone." Lachlan cast a glance at Smith.

Kinsey didn't think Smith looked much happier at that option.

"We'll work on rotation," Lachlan said, "with one of us being Kinsey's protection."

She nodded, although she hated the idea of the team being one person down as they investigated Enzo. But one look at Smith's face said he wasn't willing to debate the idea. "If I've got a laptop, I can do some of my work remotely."

"I'll hook you up, Kinse," Brooks said.

Everyone rose to leave. They cleaned up bottles and pizza boxes. Kinsey got hugs from everyone, and they shuffled out with goodbyes and waves.

"Time for bed," Smith said.

Suddenly feeling tired, Kinsey headed for the bathroom. She washed her face and pulled on her pajamas. She climbed into Smith's bed, the sheets smelling of him. She pressed her cheek against the pillow and breathed deep.

A second later, the bed moved as Hercules leaped onto it. He pressed a nose to the covers, then flopped down with a huff of air.

"Hey, boy. You going to keep me company?"

She was feeling sleepy when she heard Smith's footsteps, followed by the sound of drawers opening. Moving her head, she watched in the dim light as he stripped down to some dark, fitted boxers. Her mouth went dry.

He came toward the bed.

"Are you sleeping on the couch again?" she asked.

"No." He paused to pat Hercules before he lifted the covers, climbed in, and pulled her close.

Oh God. Heat radiated off him. He felt *so* good.

"I'm staying right beside you, Kinsey."

He pulled her closer until her cheek pressed to his chest. "Okay."

"We'll find this asshole."

"He used me." She held on to Smith tightly. "I kissed a bad guy." Thank God she wised up before she'd let Enzo talk her into bed.

"Shh. We'll find this Enzo fucker and who he works for. Then this will all be over." Smith pressed a kiss to the top of her head. "Sleep now."

Kinsey didn't think she could sleep. Not with all the turmoil inside, and the impossible-to-shake feeling that she was to blame for all of this.

But with Smith's warmth and strength wrapped around her, it was only minutes until she drifted off.

SMITH WOKE up holding an armful of warm female.

He tightened his hold on Kinsey and breathed deep, smelling the scent of her shampoo. She gave a sleepy sigh and curled into him, her cheek pressed to his bare chest, her silky hair spilling over him. Fuck, that hair gave him all kinds of fantasies. Her breath puffed across his skin. In an instant, he was as hard as a rock.

On the other side of her, Hercules stirred, eyed Smith sleepily, then leaped off the bed.

Smith kept watching her, enjoying that she looked peaceful, and that her bruises were finally fading. She stirred a little, eyelids fluttering, then settled again.

Damn, he wanted her so badly. More than he'd wanted anyone or anything before.

But he wasn't taking advantage of her. Not now. But when she was a hundred percent better...

He carefully slid out of the bed and watched as she sprawled into his spot, snuggling into his pillow.

He liked seeing her there, tucked up in his bed. That gorgeous blonde hair on his pillow.

Smith took a quick shower and dressed. He was in the kitchen, putting bread in the toaster, when she wandered out.

Her hair was pulled up in a messy bun, and the sight of her made him freeze. Those tiny pajamas left little to the imagination. All that skin, those long, long legs. She looked irresistible.

"Hey," she murmured sleepily.

"Sleep okay?"

She mumbled something in response, shuffling in his direction.

Hercules gave her a woof of welcome and galloped toward her. She gave the dog a quick, absentminded head rub.

She was so damn adorable first thing in the morning. He held up a mug of coffee.

Snatching it, she let out a little moan and took a large sip.

"Toast?"

She blinked. "You cook?"

"Not really. But I can make toast and heat things up."

Now she smiled, and it lit up her face. She moved closer, brushing against him as she peered at the toaster.

His gaze dropped to those slim legs and the scent of strawberries wafted in his direction.

She was too much temptation.

He trapped her against the counter and she went still, looking up at him. Her gaze got stuck on his chest before she finally met his gaze. She licked her lips.

Smith lowered his head and kissed her. She tasted like toothpaste, coffee, and that sweet taste that was all Kinsey. Her arms wrapped around his neck and she pressed into him, moaning as she deepened the kiss.

"No more waiting," she said. "I'm fine, Smith."

He groaned and slanted his head, sliding his tongue against hers. He cupped her sweet ass, ready to lift her onto the counter. *Yes.* He had to have her.

Suddenly, the sensor alarm blared from his phone. *Hell.*

She froze, her fingers digging into his skin. "No."

"That'll be Axel. He's your bodyguard today. I'm heading out with the team to follow up on some leads."

She made a small, frustrated sound and dropped her head to his chest. He stroked her back, feeling just as frustrated as she was.

He heard Axel at the door and stepped back.

A second later, his teammate breezed into the kitchen, Hercules bumping into him to say hello. "Morning. I'll have some toast, please. I'm starved."

Smith shot him a look, then turned to put some more bread in the toaster.

Axel stopped, looked at Kinsey, then Smith, then back at Kinsey, his gaze lingering on her bare legs. Smith barely suppressed a growl and Axel's grin was huge.

Axel sat on a stool. "How you feeling, Kinse?"

"Fine. Better."

Soon, they were all seated around the counter, eating their breakfast. Kinsey was quiet while Smith and Axel talked about the plan to hunt down Enzo Rossi.

After he was finished, Smith gathered his gear and prepared to leave.

"You guys be careful." Smith locked gazes with Axel, sending the man a warning. *Protect her.*

Axel lifted his chin.

"Is it okay if we head out?" Kinsey asked. "Your fridge is empty and we need some food. I need more than air to survive on."

Smith nodded. "Stay beside Axel. Don't go *anywhere* without him."

She nodded.

Smith moved closer and stroked her hair. "He needs to be right beside you, in touching distance."

"Okay, Smith."

"The ladies tell me this is no hardship, *chiquita*," Axel said with a wink.

A small smile tipped her lips and she rolled her eyes, then she looked back at Smith. "I can do that."

Smith stroked her hair one last time, wanting to kiss her, but not in front of Axel. Fighting a tense, edgy feeling, he headed out the door.

"Smith, wait."

He turned, and Kinsey threw herself into his arms.

The kiss was wet and deep and hot.

"I'll see you later," she murmured.

"You will, sunshine." He stroked a finger down her nose and forced himself to set her aside. He headed for his SUV.

On the drive into the city, all Smith could think of was sexy kisses and strawberries. He met the others at Lachlan's condo.

"Hey." Lachlan lifted his chin.

"How's our girl?" Blair asked.

"The bruises look better today."

Smith glanced at Lachlan, and the mess of papers spread out on the coffee table. Callie was shuffling through them, and Seth was intently looking at a tablet.

"What have we got?" Smith asked.

"Tracked down Enzo," Lachlan said. "He also goes by Enzo Russo and Enzo Romano. Has a few other aliases as well, though."

Bastard. Smith's hands flexed. He wasn't surprised.

"Blair and I checked out his apartment," Lachlan added. "Layer of dust says he hasn't been home for a while. Priority is to find him and have a chat."

Smith nodded. He definitely wanted to chat with this ass. "I need to make a few calls and finalize the security system work at Kinsey's apartment."

"Do it," Lachlan said. "Then we're going to take a look at a few places we heard Enzo likes to frequent."

Smith made his calls. He was in no rush to have the work at her apartment finished. He liked having her at his place.

"So," Blair drawled. "Have you stopped bullshitting yourself about Kinsey?"

Smith stiffened.

"Blair," Lachlan said, his voice filled with warning.

Blair shook her head. "No, we all know he's crazy

about her, and she's head over heels for him. He's holding back."

"I've got my reasons."

"Your reasons suck."

Smith shoved his hands on his hips. God save him from nosy teammates. "Don't see you embracing a healthy relationship, Blair."

"Don't turn this onto me—"

"We all have our demons. You know that." *Fuck.* Emotion churned in his gut. "She deserves a regular guy, an easy guy with no baggage. A man who can make her happy."

"She deserves the man she wants," Blair said quietly. "One of the best men I know."

Smith sucked in a breath. The others were all watching him.

Lachlan caught his gaze. "You don't heal what cut you, Smith, then you end up bleeding over the people who never hurt you." Their team leader paused. "Now, enough counselling. We have an asshole to track down."

Soon, the team climbed into the SUV and headed to the first address to check. It was a condo near the Strip belonging to a cousin of Enzo's. On the drive there, Blair and Lachlan's words kept rattling around in Smith's head.

Lila had cut him. The shit he'd waded through and seen as a SEAL had kept the wounds bloody. Losing his foot and several friends in that fucked up mission had cut even deeper.

He'd been sure the wounds had healed. But maybe they'd just scabbed over. When they reached the rundown condos, Smith forced himself to push his thoughts aside.

No one answered Lachlan's knock, so Smith rammed his shoulder against the door. The flimsy locks broke open.

Inside was a dusty mess. The team moved through, clearing the rooms.

"No one's been here in a while," Callie murmured.

There was some paperwork spread out on the table. Some were clearly photos. Smith got closer and every cell in his body went on alert. They were photos of Kinsey.

"Shit," Lachlan muttered.

With his gloved hand, Smith flicked through them. Taken with a telephoto lens. There were pictures of her shopping, stopping at the drycleaners, picking up flowers from a florist. In all of them she was smiling. Smith studied the one of her coming out of the florist. She had a bunch of sunny, yellow flowers in her arms, and was sniffing them with pure joy on her face. Smith had never bought flowers for a woman before, but he made a note that Kinsey liked yellow ones.

There were several photos of Kinsey in her apartment, taken through the window. In one, she was getting changed. *Fuckers.*

"We'll question the neighbors," Blair said. She nodded at Callie, and the women slipped out of the condo.

"You okay?" Lachlan asked.

"Yeah." He'd be better when he planted his fist in this Enzo's face.

Smith pulled out his cell, needing to hear Kinsey's voice. He punched her number. It rang and rang.

"This is Kinsey. Leave me a message, and I'll get back to you as soon as I can. Have a great day!"

From the tone of her cheery message, you could tell she was smiling. Smith frowned. She was probably in the grocery store with Axel. He'd try her again later.

Lachlan collected up the photos, sliding them into a bag. Blair and Callie returned.

"No one's seen Mancini, the cousin, or Enzo for a while," Blair said.

Smith dragged in a breath. He was in the wind. *Fuck.* He spotted another piece of paper scrunched up on the floor under the table. He grabbed it and opened it.

His gut hardened. "Guys."

They all looked. There was a logo on the paper—a circular design that looked like some sort of stylized bird.

"Same logo that was on the original note they left when they grabbed Kinsey," Lachlan said.

This time there were also words. *Cosca Unita.*

What or who the hell were Cosca Unita?

Lachlan lifted his phone. "Brooks? Sending some info through to you. Got another name for you to run. Cosca Unita. Yeah, sounds Italian. Call me as soon as you find something."

Back at the SUV, Smith slipped into the driver's seat.

"Let's check out the bar that Enzo likes to frequent," Lachlan said.

Smith nodded and pulled away from the curb. Enzo might be hiding, but Smith was a damn good hunter and he always got his prey.

CHAPTER NINE

K insey pulled some cans off the shelf, tossing them in the shopping cart. Axel was pushing, his forearms resting on the handle. He looked bored.

"Sorry you got stuck with me today," she said.

His soulful brown eyes flicked to her. "Hardly a chore, *chiquita*."

She smiled and grabbed a bag of pasta.

"Kinse, you've got enough food here to feed an army."

"Smith's cupboards are bare."

"I think *mi amigo* chews on nails and wood for sustenance."

A laugh burst out of her, and she flashed Axel a look. He returned it with a sexy, wide smile.

Kinsey looked back to the shelves. She wanted to cook Smith a nice dinner. She wasn't a gourmet chef or anything, but she liked to cook. She'd grown up scraping together whatever she could, usually peanut butter and jelly sandwiches. More often than not, she'd gone hungry.

Once she'd escaped and come to Las Vegas, she vowed she'd never eat another PB&J again. So she'd learned to cook some decent meals, and she enjoyed it.

She wandered farther down the aisle, when she felt fingers on the back of her shirt.

"Stay close, Kinsey."

The easy charm was gone and Axel's face was deadly serious. She could see the former Delta Force soldier shining through.

"You don't leave my side," he reminded her.

She nodded. Soon, they headed toward the checkout.

The young woman serving them flashed Axel plenty of smiles. He ignored her, but Kinsey was certain Axel was used to every woman over the age of five batting her eyelashes at him. He just radiated sex appeal and charm.

Kinsey started stacking bags in the cart. When she pulled out her wallet to pay, Axel gave her a hard look. She raised her hands. She wasn't going to argue with a macho military man if he was intent on paying the grocery bill.

She turned, looking out the plate glass windows into the parking lot.

Her gaze snagged on a heavily-pregnant woman crossing the lot. Suddenly, the woman stumbled, clutching at her rounded belly.

Kinsey stiffened. Something was wrong. Then she saw a car come around the corner, driving too fast, and heading straight toward the pregnant woman.

Get off the road. Move. The woman spasmed and doubled over.

Oh, no. Without a single thought, Kinsey ran. She sprinted for the door, heard Axel shout behind her.

She raced into the parking lot and toward the woman. She waved her arms at the oncoming car and it swerved.

"Hang on." Kinsey reached the pregnant lady, grabbing her arm. "Take it easy. You're okay."

The woman's face was scrunched in pain. Then she looked up at Kinsey's face and her features smoothed out.

The woman lifted something and jammed it against Kinsey's side.

What the hell? Kinsey felt a jolt rock through her. Her legs went out from under her and she fell to her knees. *Ow.* She grabbed the woman reflexively, her hands gripping the woman's belly.

That's when the woman's "belly" slid to the side.

It was fake. The woman wasn't really pregnant. A trick, and Kinsey had fallen for it.

So stupid.

The woman leaned over, she was smiling. Anger ignited and Kinsey swung out. Her fist connected with the woman's nose.

"Shit." The woman staggered back, clutching her face. Then she jabbed her arm forward.

Pain flashed through Kinsey again and she pitched forward. Stun gun. Her limbs were twitching. Her cheek hit the pavement and she saw Axel sprinting toward her with powerful strides.

Then Kinsey heard gunfire.

Axel's body jerked and blood bloomed on his shoulder.

No! He went down on one knee and she saw three big men, all armed, racing toward him. Axel lifted his gun and started firing. She tried to push up, but none of her muscles obeyed her.

One man went down, but then the other two were on him. Kinsey blinked slowly, watching the fight erupt into hard punches and kicks that made her wince. Axel gave as good as he got, laying out a second man, but the final man kicked him hard, and Axel went down.

No. No. No! She watched Axel slump to the ground. She had to do *something*, but she couldn't move.

She heard an engine and a van pulled up right in front of them. The "pregnant" woman yanked the side door open.

Dammit to hell. She was being kidnapped. *Again.*

She saw two men dragging Axel closer. *Think, Kinse!* She glanced upward, staring right at the van's license plate. An idea struck her. She managed to move one hand just enough to grab hold of a small rock.

Painfully aware that the clock was ticking, Kinsey gritted her teeth and started scraping the letters and numbers of the license plate onto the asphalt.

But she hadn't gotten far when hands grabbed her, and she was dragged off the ground. She was tossed in the van, and a second later, Axel was dropped onto the floor beside her. He wasn't moving and his T-shirt was covered in blood. Her heart clenched.

She was pretty sure Smith was going to be really, really mad about this.

"That bitch broke my nose!" The fake-pregnant lady was holding a cloth to her nose.

The van pulled out, fast. Kinsey was tossed against her seat.

Kinsey glared at the whining woman, and then noticed another man sitting in the van. Kinsey blinked. He was dressed in the style of a Tibetan monk, clothed in maroon and saffron-colored robes. His dark eyes met hers, his expression calm.

He had a black eye, so she guessed he wasn't here by choice.

Kinsey drew in a breath. "My friend's bleeding, he needs help—"

"Shut up," the woman snapped. "I don't care if he bleeds to death."

Kinsey looked away, and her gaze fell on a familiar, matte-black box at the back of the van.

"That doesn't work," a voice said.

Her head snapped up. She knew that voice. She saw Enzo duck in from the front of the van. He stabbed a finger at the box.

"You asshole!" Kinsey lost it, and launched herself up at him. She aimed her nails for his face.

Fake-pregnant woman yanked her back.

Enzo was handsome, his dark hair flopping over his forehead, in need of a cut. He was slim and lean, and now she knew he was also a complete asshole.

He smiled at her. "Hi, Kinse."

She spat at him, enjoying when he leaped back and scowled at her.

He held up a hand. "Please calm down, sweetheart."

"Do *not* call me that."

The woman shook her. "How do we work the artifact?"

"I have no idea," Kinsey said. "And nor does he." She pointed at the unconscious Axel. *Be okay, Axel, please.*

"This guy—" Enzo pointed at the monk "—can't get it to work, either."

That's when the fake-pregnant lady pulled out a handgun. She pointed it at the monk's head, and Kinsey sucked in a breath.

"We don't need you guys, then," the woman said. "I'll shoot him first and then your friend." She toed Axel with her boot.

"No." Kinsey surged forward, trying to cover Axel with her body. "The artifact is a fake. They didn't give you the real one."

Curses filled the van.

The woman moved, sinking a hand into Kinsey's hair. She yanked Kinsey up so hard her scalp burned. "Now we're getting somewhere."

"Lenore, take it easy," Enzo implored.

"Shut up." The woman wrenched Kinsey's head back, tugging on her hair. Then she smiled, and the expression made Kinsey's blood go cold. "I have a plan I think will get us exactly what we need."

SITTING IN THE SUV, Smith tried Kinsey's phone again. Blair was driving them to their next location. So far, they hadn't found any sign of Enzo Rossi.

"This is Kinsey. Leave me a message—"

He ended the call and tried Axel's phone. No answer. He tried them both again, not liking the prickle on the back of his neck.

Then Lachlan's phone rang.

In the backseat, Lachlan pressed his phone to his ear. "Hunter."

Smith saw his friend's expression change, and ice slid into his veins.

Lachlan nodded. "We'll meet you there. Thanks, MacKade."

Shit. Smith watched Lachlan slide his phone away.

"There's been a report of an attack at the Albertsons on Blue Diamond Road."

Smith's chin dropped to his chest. That was close to his place. "Fuck."

"Eyewitnesses reported that a man and a woman were snatched and dragged into a van."

"Let's go," Smith ground out.

With a nod, Blair steered the SUV into a sharp turn.

As they drove, Smith stared out the windshield, trying to lock down his rage and worry. But every minute of the drive felt like an hour, scraping his nerves raw.

Finally, they screeched into the parking lot of the grocery store. Several police cruisers were parked haphazardly near the entrance, and there were cops talking with some bystanders. MacKade was there, standing a head taller than everyone else.

Before Blair had even stopped the SUV, Smith swung open his door and jumped out.

MacKade nodded at him.

"What the hell happened?" Smith demanded.

"Perps lured your girl out of the store—"

"She came out alone?" Smith's jaw clenched. He sensed his team step up beside him.

MacKade held up a phone. "This is from the store's security camera." He tilted the screen so they could see.

Smith peered at a grainy video of a pregnant woman doubling over in the parking lot. A second later, Kinsey rushed out of the store to help. Grimly, he watched the pregnant woman attack Kinsey and stun her.

"Those fuckers," Seth bit off from behind Smith.

Smith felt the same. They'd used Kinsey's goodness against her.

"She got in a good punch," Blair said.

Next, they watched Axel sprinting out of the store. When he got shot, all of Team 52 sucked in sharp breaths. They all watched the brutal fight that followed, along with Kinsey and Axel being dragged into the white van.

"Your man left us a dead body." The police detective pointed to a nearby body bag laid out beside one of the cruisers. "No ID yet. Your guy looked like he injured the others, but he took a bullet."

Lachlan lifted his phone. "Brooks, they were taken in a white van." Lachlan repeated the make and model, then looked at MacKade. "Plate?"

MacKade shook his head. "No clear shot of it in the video, and none of the witnesses thought to note it down."

Dammit. Smith glanced around the parking lot. There were probably a million of those white vans in

Vegas. He strode to the spot where Kinsey had fallen. He stood there, hands on his hips.

He'd failed her. He'd promised to keep her safe and he'd failed her.

He saw the abduction happen again in his head, move by move. There was nothing in the security feed that would help him find her.

"Smith?" Lachlan's concerned voice. His teammates circled around him.

"I'm fine."

Smith looked at the ground, picturing Kinsey sprawled there, in pain. Then he spotted the faint, white scratch marks on the pavement. He frowned and crouched.

Kinsey would have been lying right here, hurting and afraid.

The markings looked like...

Well, damn. "552 P."

"What's that?" MacKade asked with a frown.

"My woman gave us a partial plate." *Good work, smart girl.*

MacKade tilted his head, studying the ground. "Hell." He swiveled to the nearby uniforms, barking out orders for them to find the van.

Lachlan called Brooks again. "We got a partial plate. Find that van, Brooks."

Smith sucked in a deep breath. Once again, Kinsey was in danger. If the bastards hurt her...

"We'll find them." Lachlan was watching him. "We'll bring her home."

"Told her I'd keep her safe." And here he was, unable

to do anything to find her except wait. A muscle worked in his jaw, his temper writhing.

"Axel was with her. We all underestimated what these bastards would do."

"Who the fuck are they?"

Lachlan scanned the parking lot. "We won't stop until we find out and take them down."

"Guys." Brooks voice came through the comm line and they all straightened.

Smith's pulse jumped.

"What have you got, Brooks?" Lachlan demanded.

"I've got the van! Just showed up on a traffic cam. They're on the beltway, headed north."

Smith turned, sprinting for the SUV. "Let's move!"

CHAPTER TEN

S mith roared onto the Las Vegas Beltway.

"Take it easy." Lachlan sat beside him in the passenger seat, one hand pressed to the roof.

Smith was not holding on or slowing down. He had to get to Kinsey.

In the backseat, Seth, Callie, and Blair sat, tense and ready.

"You're about a mile behind them." Brooks' voice came through on the dash. The large screen built into the center console showed a glowing dot moving along the beltway.

Smith moved into the next lane, speeding past a truck. *I'm coming, Kinsey.*

"Guys, I got some more info on Cosca Unita," Brooks said.

Smith roared around another car, his gut tightening. "Spill it."

Brooks sighed. "They look like some militant Mafia

group. Recently formed, but working to make a name for themselves. Cosca is Italian, meaning clan or family. Sicilian Mafia used it for crime family units run by a capo."

Blair leaned forward. "And unita?"

"Means united."

"United Family," Lachlan murmured. "What do they want?"

"Money. Power. I haven't found much more on them yet."

"How the hell did they know about the artifact and that we had it?" Blair said. "Even if they were spying on Kinsey, they still had to know about Area 52 first."

"I think I might have an answer for that as well," Brooks said. "Nat did some digging. Remember the U.S. military team that was given the artifact by the monks?"

"Yeah," Lachlan prompted.

"One of the soldiers was an Italian-American by the name of Vincent Salvatore. Upstanding soldier, but had links to family members who were not so upstanding."

Lachlan cursed. "And Vinny probably shared a few tales in his old age."

"There's the van." Smith spotted the white van ahead and put his foot down on the accelerator.

They sped up behind the van.

But the driver saw them coming. The van shot forward.

No, you don't. Smith gave chase. He whipped their SUV into the neighboring lane. They zoomed up beside the van.

The driver glanced their way, before looking forward

again. Lachlan lowered his window and aimed his SIG. The driver looked again, his eyes widening.

"We don't want them to crash," Smith said. They had no idea if Kinsey and Axel were strapped in.

Lachlan fired.

The bullets pinged on metal. The van swerved toward them.

Fuck. Smith yanked the wheel to avoid the van, then righted them.

"Cars ahead," Callie yelled.

Smith looked up and saw several cars in front of the van. The van driver swerved again, but clipped the edge of one car. The car spun away, tires screeching, hitting another car.

"Shit," Blair said.

Callie looked back. "Don't think anyone was hurt."

Blair wrinkled her nose. "MacKade's going to hear about it, though."

"Blair, get out the urchins," Lachlan ordered.

With a smile, Blair leaned into the very back of the SUV. "Ty will be happy to hear we're going to use these babies."

In the rearview mirror, Smith saw Blair settle back into her seat. She was clutching two black balls the size of tennis balls.

The devices were Ty's invention. They were attracted to rubber and once they stuck to a tire, spikes exploded out of them.

Blair lowered her window and half climbed out of the window. "Get us closer!"

Smith accelerated, pulling up close to the van. *Hang on, Kinsey.*

Blair tossed the first urchin, then the second one. She had a hell of an arm.

Bang. Bang.

The van swerved like crazy, out of control. With a curse, Smith slowed and pulled back. The van cut across the lanes.

Shit. The driver hadn't slowed down. They were going too fast.

The van smashed into the concrete wall at the edge of the beltway with a deafening crunch of metal. The back end of the van lifted off the ground before crashing back down.

Smith slammed on the brakes. The SUV's tires screeched as he pulled them to a halt nearby.

"Callie, Seth, control the traffic." Lachlan pushed open his door.

Leaping out of the vehicle, Smith grabbed his CXM. He moved in beside Lachlan and Blair, both of them with their assault rifles up and aimed.

Lachlan moved to the front of the van. "Driver's dead."

Blair gripped the side door, her bi-colored gaze meeting Smith's. His pulse was pounding. He kept his weapon aimed and nodded.

She yanked the door open.

Smith cursed.

The back of the van was empty.

"Fuck!" He turned and slammed a fist into the side of the van, denting the panel.

Lachlan stepped up beside him. "They must have dropped them somewhere or swapped them to another vehicle."

Smith turned, staring blindly across the lanes of the beltway. *Where was she?*

Lachlan touched his ear. "Brooks, the van is empty."

"Shit," came the man's response. "Well, I have news."

The tone of Brooks' voice made Smith's gut tighten.

Lachlan dragged in a breath and looked at the team. "Go ahead."

Smith waited, muscles tense. *Please. Kinsey had to be okay.*

"A package was delivered to the Bunker...by a man matching Enzo Rossi's description."

Smith's jaw locked. "I'm driving."

No one argued with him. They jumped into the SUV, Lachlan directing Brooks to report the crashed van to MacKade. Smith broke the speed limit on the way to the Bunker, but he didn't care.

They sped back down the beltway, then exited at the airport. They passed through security and pulled up in front of the squat, concrete building. His gaze fell on the box resting in front of the door.

As they neared, Callie pulled out a small device and held it up near the box. "Not registering for explosives."

"Bring it inside," Lachlan ordered.

Smith grabbed it and carried it in. It didn't weigh much. Someone flicked the lights on, and he set the box down on Kinsey's desk.

His heart was pounding.

Lachlan stepped forward and flicked open a knife.

He cut the box open and quickly lifted the lid. When he looked inside, his face paled.

Fuck. Air lodged in his lungs, Smith shouldered forward.

Lachlan grabbed his arm. "Smith—"

Smith couldn't breathe. He flung the sides of the box open.

Blindly, he stared at the luscious golden locks of hair inside. A mass of it.

Beautiful hair he knew so well. Kinsey's hair.

They'd shorn her fucking hair off.

Blair shifted. "Dammit to hell."

Seth growled. Callie pulled in a deep breath.

Smith reached in and grabbed the note nestled in the hair.

Meet us at Lorenzi Park with the real artifact in one hour. If you're late, we'll send you her finger next. For every hour you don't show up, you'll get another body part. His ear, her eye, his tongue.

That damn bird logo was stamped on the bottom. Smith pressed his hands to the back of his neck. *Shit.*

"We don't have time to come up with a plan," Blair said.

Lachlan shook his head. "They planned it that way. Brooks, get Jonah on the line. And tell Arlo to get the real artifact here. Fast."

Smith looked up, staring at Lachlan.

His leader's eyes glittered. "We're going to save them." Lachlan's voice was hard, firm.

Calm descended on Smith. Kinsey and Axel needed him to keep his shit together. "Hell, yeah."

THEY WERE LOCKED IN A SMALL, dark room.

Again, Kinsey checked Axel. He still hadn't regained consciousness. The bleeding had slowed, but it hadn't stopped. She kept the ragged ball of fabric pressed to his shoulder.

"Please wake up, Axel," she murmured for what felt like the hundredth time.

She'd torn the bottom of her T-shirt off, which was *way* harder to do in real life than in the movies. Her hands were covered in his blood.

"You're okay, Tenzin?" she asked over her shoulder.

The monk nodded. They'd talked a little after they'd been tossed in this room. He'd been snatched from in front of a Buddhist temple in Los Angeles.

Kinsey touched her raggedly cut hair. That bitch had not been gentle when she'd sheared it off. Instead of reaching her shoulders, her hair now tickled her jaw in a jagged bob. Still, it was the least of Kinsey's worries right now.

She knew Smith and the others would be working to find them. She just had to hold on. Her breath hitched at the thought. Smith would be out of his mind.

The door opened, and Enzo was standing in the doorway. She glared at him.

"Come on." He grabbed her arm and pulled her up.

She kicked at him, but he dodged.

"Behave. I don't want you to get hurt, Kinsey."

"You're a dickhead."

His lips pressed into a flat line. "Don't make this harder than it needs to be."

"Oh, I have no desire to make this easy for you."

"Enzo, quit screwing around," another man called out.

She watched a pair of men stride past and drag Axel off the floor. They weren't gentle.

"Be careful! He's hurt."

The men ignored her.

"Move it, monk," one barked at Tenzin.

The monk rose and followed.

They were led into an elevator, and soon they were walking across a parking garage. There weren't many cars in the place. They were loaded into the back of a nondescript sedan. Axel was dropped on the floor at her feet, and Kinsey bit her lip.

The next thing she knew, one of the men pulled a blindfold over her eyes. Next, her wrists were bound together.

"I'm so glad I never let you get too far with me," she snapped at Enzo. "You're trash."

"Kinsey..." His voice sounded almost regretful. "I never wanted—"

The engine started with a rumble, cutting Enzo off. The car started to move in reverse. Soon, she guessed they were out on the street, heading...somewhere. What was happening now?

Her thoughts turned to Smith. Big, strong Smith. He had to be coming. God, she hoped he was coming.

She wasn't sure how much time had passed. Ten

minutes? Maybe fifteen. The car stopped, and the doors opened. She sat there, tense. She pressed her hands to Axel's shoulder. He still hadn't moved. Everything was quiet.

"What's happening?" She hated the tremor in her voice.

She didn't get an answer.

"Tenzin?"

"I'm here, Ms. Kinsey."

Kinsey could hear birds tweeting from outside the car. *Screw this.* She awkwardly pushed her blindfold up with her bound hands. Tenzin was sitting beside her, also blindfolded. Apart from Axel sprawled on the floor, no one else was in the vehicle.

She leaned forward and pressed her tied hands to Axel's neck. She felt his pulse beat against the side of her hand. Thankfully, it was strong.

She brushed the hair off his face, and suddenly she felt like crying. But she sucked the tears back. She knew from experience they didn't help.

Instead, she vowed revenge on Enzo and his band of douchebags.

Suddenly, she heard deep voices nearby, and she quickly slipped the blindfold back down. Trying to keep her breathing calm, she listened. The door beside her opened and she froze.

She'd fight. She was done being the victim.

Sensing somebody close to her, Kinsey launched herself at whoever the hell it was. She swung her bound hands.

They were caught by strong fingers.

"Kinsey."

It was Smith's deep voice.

Air caught in her chest and suddenly her blindfold was gone. She blinked, seeing Smith's rugged face and the rest of Team 52 behind him.

"Thank God," she said. "Axel's hurt."

Smith moved, pulling her closer. His mouth hit hers for a hard, quick kiss. She kissed him back.

"You're okay?" He pulled her out of the car.

"I'm fine, but Axel's unconscious. He's got a gunshot wound—" Her voice broke.

"Get him out of the vehicle," Callie called out.

Lachlan and Seth pulled Axel out of the car, laying him on the grass.

Smith pulled a knife off his belt and sliced through her bindings. Kinsey looked around and noticed they were in a park.

"And this is Tenzin," she said, as Blair helped the monk from the car. "He was kidnapped by Enzo and those guys as well."

The monk nodded at them. "Thank you for freeing us."

Kinsey watched as Callie worked on Axel, giving him an injection and setting to work on his bullet wound.

"His vitals are strong," Callie said. "Looks like he's got a concussion. When we get back, I'll remove the bullet, then he'll need some rest."

Kinsey tipped her head up to Smith. "How did you find us?"

He reached out, brushing her shorn hair. "We got the message you left us. The van's plate."

She heard the pride in his voice and she smiled.

Then he touched her hair again, something dark working in his eyes. "And then Enzo sent us a message."

"It'll grow back," she whispered.

A muscle worked in Smith's jaw, and he managed a nod.

"I'm so glad you found us. Did you catch Enzo and the others?"

Now Smith's face turned grim.

Kinsey stilled, glancing around at the others. They all had similar looks on their faces.

A chill went down her spine. "What happened?"

"They gave us an ultimatum. The real artifact in return for you and Axel," Lachlan said.

Kinsey sucked in a breath, her fingers digging into Smith's arm. "No."

Smith nodded. "They have the real artifact, but the most important thing is that you're safe."

As he hugged her, she held on tight.

But even Smith's arms couldn't obliterate the sense of impending doom.

BACK AT THE BUNKER, Smith opened the SUV door and helped Kinsey out.

He slid an arm around her and then lifted her off her feet. He carried her inside.

"I can walk," she said.

"No."

She was breathing and alive. He kept having to remind himself. She had no new injuries, but right then, he decided he was keeping her as close as he could.

In his arms.

"Is Tenzin okay?" she asked.

"Yeah. Lachlan arranged for him to be dropped off at a local Buddhist temple. They'll arrange for him to get back to L.A."

Smith headed into the hangar. Seth and Lachlan followed, carrying Axel on a stretcher. Blair and Callie brought up the rear. Axel had stirred a little on the drive to the Bunker. He'd said a few words, but was clearly confused. Callie was monitoring him, and once they were back at base, she'd treat his other injuries.

Smith climbed into the X8.

"Wait...I thought it crashed," Kinsey said, confused.

"This is our backup." Arlo appeared from the cockpit, the older man looking grumpy as usual. His gaze fell on Kinsey. "Heard you got yourself kidnapped."

"Um..."

"And Creed went rogue, tearing through the desert to save you."

"Well, that's what he does," she said.

Arlo grunted. "And then you got kidnapped again."

"Unfortunately, yes."

Another grunt. "Don't do it again."

"Arlo," Smith growled.

Kinsey shot the man a weak smile. "Believe me, it isn't high on my To Do list."

Blair bumped her shoulder against the older man as she moved into the cockpit. "I'm flying now, old man."

Arlo growled. "I'll show you old."

Callie got the stretcher settled at the back of the aircraft, strapping into a seat closest to Axel.

Smith sat, pulling Kinsey into his lap.

"Smith—"

"You're not moving."

She stared into his face. "I'm all right."

"I know. And I'll believe it soon."

With a sigh, she relaxed into him. Soon, they were airborne for the short flight to Area 52.

Once they arrived, he was damn glad to lead her inside. She'd be safe in the secure base.

"Kinse." Brooks rushed out to meet them, worry on his handsome face. "You had us all worried."

"Thanks, Brooks."

"All right, planning meeting," Lachlan said. "We have an artifact to recover."

Kinsey's shoulders drooped. "I'm so sorry about the artifact. If I hadn't rushed out to help that woman—"

"Then you wouldn't be you." Smith curled his hands around her shoulders. "No one is blaming you."

She glanced over at Axel on the stretcher. "I'm blaming me. It's my fault he's hurt."

Smith shook his head. "No. It's the fuckers who hurt him. It's their fault."

Taking her arm, Smith led her into the rec room and nudged her into a chair. She needed something to help her relax. He knew she liked tea, so he went about making her a cup.

When he set the steaming cup down in front of her, she blinked. Then she graced him with a tiny smile.

At that moment, Jonah strode in.

Kinsey looked up at the director. "I'm so sorry—"

Smith growled. He was sick of all her apologies for things that weren't her fault.

Jonah held up a hand, stopping her mid-sentence. "You are not to blame, Kinsey."

"I keep trying to tell her that," Smith said.

"Your job carries some risk," Jonah said. "And I'm sorry for everything that's happened to you."

She swallowed. "The artifact—?"

Jonah's hawkish face hardened. "We'll get it back."

Brooks strode in with the rest of the team. The computer guru grabbed an energy drink from the refrigerator, his gaze on his tablet the entire time.

"I found more info on Cosca Unita." Brooks smiled grimly. "Found it on the dark web."

"What do they want?" Kinsey asked.

"No government. They want to return to a feudal time, where the most powerful take what they want and rule their own little kingdoms."

Smith leaned a hip against the table. "You're shitting me."

"Unfortunately, no. I'm still trying to find more info on where and how they operate."

Kinsey set her tea down, suddenly feeling nauseated. "They want to destroy the world, and they have a dangerous artifact."

"Like I said," Jonah said. "We'll get it back. It's what we do."

"How?" Kinsey asked.

"We'll reach out to our contacts," Jonah said. "Brooks will keep searching."

Smith knew what they weren't saying. The best chance to find the artifact was when Cosca Unita used the damn thing.

But Kinsey had been through enough for today. "Come on." He gripped her shoulder. "Time for you to get some rest."

She nodded. "Can we check on Axel first?"

"Anything you want, sunshine."

CHAPTER ELEVEN

K insey had to jog a little to keep up with Smith's long strides as he led her down the hall to his quarters. There was an intense vibe radiating off him, so she didn't talk.

Besides, for all his reassurances, she was still worried about Axel and the artifact. Everything that had happened continued to ricochet around in her head.

Axel had woken when they'd visited him in the infirmary. Callie had patched him up and just as they were about to leave, Natalie had arrived. The normally impeccably dressed and groomed archeologist had looked disheveled and panicked. Her black hair had been loose and her gorgeous face pinched with stress.

Kinsey had seen the fear in the woman's eyes before she'd hidden it. She'd then started bossing Axel about getting some rest, and the man had rallied enough to snap unhappily at her. Smith and Kinsey had left the pair sniping at each other.

Smith stopped and opened a door. "Come on in."

She ducked in and headed straight for the bathroom. When she looked in the mirror and she saw her hair, she winced. She'd loved her hair. It was the one thing even her mama had commented on and said was beautiful.

Kinsey pulled in a breath. It wasn't too bad, but it definitely needed a cut to tidy it up. She bit her lip and reminded herself yet again that it would grow back.

Smith stepped in front of her, cutting off her view, and started unbuttoning her shirt. Methodically, like a man on a mission, he stripped her clothes off.

She swallowed. He was staring at her, watching every part of her that he uncovered. When she looked up into his face, she saw that his eyes were alive with emotion.

Kinsey found it hard to breathe.

"Smith?"

He turned away, switching on the shower. Once the steam was rising, he nudged her inside. As soon as the warm water hit her, she closed her eyes and swallowed a moan. It felt so good.

She heard the rustling of clothes and opened her eyes. Through the glass, she saw Smith stripping off his own gear.

Her heart stuttered. *God.*

He was big. So big. That broad chest she'd admired so many times with its smattering of dark hair. Heavy abs that her fingers itched to explore. She wanted to touch every dip and ridge.

Then he unfastened his trousers and kicked them off. *Oh. Wow.*

He had long, solid legs with muscular thighs. And a long, heavy cock.

He was beautiful. Pure beauty in a masculine, powerful way.

Pulling the door open, he stepped into the shower. As soon as he was inside, it made the space feel tiny. He towered over Kinsey and her body tingled—she was so very aware of him. Reaching behind her, he grabbed the shower gel and squeezed some onto his palms. Then he cupped her shoulders and started soaping her skin.

"Done denying what we both want, Kinsey."

A shiver moved through her. *Finally.*

"You're mine now. Not letting you get away."

A crisp, pine scent filled the air. *Oh, God.* Smith's hands were big and rough. As they moved over her, slicking down her shoulders and arms, she felt the tantalizing calluses on his fingers. His hands moved down her back, and then to the front again, to cup her breasts.

"So fucking gorgeous." His voice was a deep growl.

Smith spun her around so her back was pressed tight to his front. Those hands kept moving over her breasts, his fingers tugging on her nipples.

Drowning in sensation, Kinsey bit her lip. She felt his heavy cock nudging her lower back, and couldn't control the small shimmy of her body.

His hands moved down, splaying over her belly. Then, before she could process what he had planned, he spun her again, pushing her back a couple of steps until her shoulder blades hit cool tile.

He dropped to his knees and she sucked in a breath. His hands skimmed down her legs.

Then they paused at her ankles and he looked up at her. His wet hair was slicked back against his head. "You want this, Kinsey? You want me?"

She nodded.

"Tell me." His hands moved up over her calves, to her knees. "You want my mouth on you, and then after, my cock inside you?"

"Yes." She didn't even need to think.

His hands kneaded her thighs, sending sparks of sensation through her. Then he pushed them apart and his fingers stroked between her legs.

She jerked. "Smith—"

"Just relax, Kinsey. I'm going to take care of you."

Those words arrowed into her heart.

He stroked her, his hands soapy and slippery. His thumb brushed her clit and she bucked.

"So responsive," he said. "I love it."

Then one thick finger slid inside her, followed by another. He lowered his head, his mouth joining the sensations.

So much. Too much. Not enough.

He worked those fingers inside her without mercy, and his tongue caressed her clit. Her cries echoed off the tiles.

She grabbed his hair. "Smith."

"Come, sunshine. I feel your body tightening around my fingers. Let go."

She did, her head flying back, pleasure washing over her like the spill of the water. "Oh, God, oh, God, oh, God...Smith."

When her legs buckled, he caught her. He pulled her

against his hot body, and then urged her under the spray. She felt him grab something, and then his hands were in her hair. He massaged her scalp, working the shampoo into her now shorter hair.

She felt his fingers slow in their movements, running through the short strands. She knew he was studying it and she felt something very unhappy throbbing off him.

Her throat tightened. "Does it look that terrible?"

"Not at all. I just hate knowing this was done to you, without your permission."

"It'll grow back, Smith."

He grunted, and his fingers started working the shampoo again. Then he rinsed her off and cut the water. He scooped her up, carrying her out of the shower like she was precious.

Setting her down on the mat, he took his time toweling her off. That meant she got to study his big, very naked body.

God, that body of his. She wanted it so badly.

Despite her amazing orgasm in the shower, desire ignited. With every stroke of the towel, and every flex of his muscles, need thrummed through her. And she was pretty sure he was going to tuck her up in bed and tell her to rest.

He wrapped the towel around her, then grabbed a second one off the rack. She watched him swipe it over his chest. He wrapped it around his waist, and then spun her to face the door. They exited the bathroom, and soon were standing right next to his bunk.

"Kinsey, you should—"

Screw this. She knew what she needed. She spun, colliding with his body. She shoved him.

Clearly, she'd caught him by surprise, because the back of his knees hit the bed and he went down. She tumbled on top of him.

SURPRISED FOR A SECOND, Smith looked up at Kinsey. She was stronger than he'd guessed.

Then her towel slipped and his thoughts flew away. He stared at the pretty pink breasts right in front of him.

"I need you, Smith."

He was trying to take care of her, dammit. "Kinsey—"

She shook her head, gripped her towel, and tossed it away. She moved, settling her slim legs so that she straddled his body. He felt the damp warmth between her thighs rub against his belly.

He groaned. Fuck, he'd never seen anything prettier or sexier.

He pulled himself together enough to find his voice. "You should r—"

"If you say rest..." she growled the words "...I'll..."

As her voice petered out, he raised a brow. "You'll what?"

She lifted her chin, pressing her palms to his chest. "I don't know. All I know is that people keep kidnapping me, and this time, I'm taking what *I* want." She thumped a fist against her chest and her breasts jiggled.

Smith's gaze went to those nipples. Shit. He wanted his mouth on her, her husky cries echoing in his ears. He wanted to slide his throbbing cock in her warmth.

"What do you want, Kinsey?" he murmured.

She licked her lips. "You. It's always been you."

His control, already worn thin by months of denial and by her being in danger, snapped.

Smith sat up, taking her mouth with his. She moaned —the kiss deep and eager.

No games from Kinsey. She wanted him and she showed it. Her nails bit into his shoulders, her body rocking against him.

Then her hands moved over his chest, down to his abs. She pulled back a little, watching the path of her hands.

Fuck. There was raw desire on her face. He'd had women hungry for his body before, but the look on Kinsey's face—it was wonder, awe.

"I love your body, Smith," she murmured. "So big, so strong."

Her hands stroked lower, and she shifted to the side. Her hands skated around where he wanted them most, her nails raking over his thighs.

When her fingers brushed where his prosthetic met skin, he stilled. Women had all kinds of reactions to it— morbid curiosity, revulsion, and some just studiously ignored it. Kinsey did none of those things. Her fingers touched the cool metal.

"Does it hurt?"

Of course, Kinsey thought of him, not herself. "No."

"Ty is a genius." She smiled. "Don't tell him, though. The man doesn't need his ego stroked." Her hands slid

133

upward and this time, she shifted to straddle Smith's thighs.

That was it. Kinsey just saw it as a part of him, like everything else. A second later, her hands closed around his cock, and his thoughts scattered.

Smith groaned, his hips jerking upward.

"I want you inside me," she breathed.

"So take me." He reached out an arm to the night-stand beside the bed. A second later, he handed her the small, foil package.

This was for her. Her choice.

Her eyes lit and she took it eagerly. She tore it open and quickly rolled the condom on him. Smith smothered a groan. Then she rose, lifting her hips. Their gazes connected as she sank down, taking his cock inside her.

"Oh." Her eyes widened.

"Relax." He knew he was a big guy. "You can take me."

She took her time, sinking down and taking him steadily inside her. She bit her lip, her hands digging into his shoulders

Finally, he was lodged deep inside her. To the hilt inside Kinsey.

Then she went wild.

She started riding him, rising and falling. "So good."

Damn, she was right. It was so fucking good. She was warm, wet, and tight. Pure heaven.

She rose and fell, her pace fast and needy. Smith gripped her hips, helping her on.

She felt so damn good. And watching her face, as she

was so lost in fucking him, was pure torture. She was riding his cock and finding her pleasure.

"Smith!"

She came alive for him and he couldn't look away. Pure beauty and sunshine. That was his Kinsey.

He slid one hand down to cup her ass, digging in and helping her move. She made the sexiest little sounds he'd ever heard. He felt the muscles at the base of his spine tightening, and knew his own release was coming in fast.

But he needed her to come again first.

Smith slid his other hand between their bodies, touching where she was stretched around him. She bucked wildly.

"Oh!"

"Love this, sunshine." He stroked again. "Us, connected."

She ground down harder on him with a husky mewl.

"Get there." He found her clit and rolled it.

Kinsey detonated, crying out his name. Her body shook, her inner muscles clamping down on his cock.

Smith reared up and flipped over, slamming her onto the bed on her back.

He hammered inside her, need riding him hard.

He needed her. Wanted to fucking absorb her until there was nothing between them, no space between Smith and Kinsey.

Her orgasm shuddered through her, and Smith thrust again, deep, coming hard. His orgasm hit him in a blinding rush.

Smith collapsed on her and knew he had to be heavy,

but her arms and legs wrapped around him tightly. Like she never wanted to let him go.

She made a sound of pure satisfaction. "That was *way* better than resting."

A laugh rumbled through Smith. He nuzzled her neck, rolling to the side and pulling her close. "Damn straight."

Bright-blue eyes looked up at him. "So when can we do it again?"

"Kinsey—"

She pressed her face to his chest. "I've wanted to do that with you forever. I have some pretty detailed fantasies."

He rolled her beneath him, unbelievably feeling his cock respond. "Really?"

She smiled, lifting her head to kiss him. "Really."

Smith let himself sink into her sunshine.

CHAPTER TWELVE

K insey woke curled into Smith's body. His arms were locked around her, and her face was pressed against his chest. She looked at her hand on his torso, admiring the contrast between his bronze skin and her lighter tone.

Smith kept her close. He'd done it all night, even in his sleep.

She loved it.

She was pretty sure she was half in love with him.

Kinsey's heart beat hard and steady. She looked at his rugged, tough face. Even in sleep, he was still the badass mountain man. How could she not fall for him?

Looking at him, and remembering all the delicious things they'd done to each other, had desire igniting low in her belly. It didn't matter that after their first spectacular time together, he'd taken her again. Slower, but no less intense.

She needed him. Now. Again. She wanted him moving over her, that big cock working inside her...

She shivered, desire flaring, and she felt a rush of damp heat between her legs. She gently stroked his chest. All those interesting ridges and slabs of muscle. She scooted lower, sliding down his body, finding that heavy cock resting on his thigh.

Kinsey licked her lips. She reached down and stroked him, watching his cock thicken and lengthen.

She moved down more, lowered her head, and licked. Mmm. She loved the feel of him, the purely male scent. She kept licking, and then felt his body tense.

"Fuck me," he growled.

She glanced up and saw Smith watching her, stark pleasure on his face.

"Hey," she said.

"Best morning wakeup ever, sunshine."

"I'm just getting started." She stroked him. "Can I—?"

"Hell, yeah."

Eagerly, Kinsey set to work, sucking him into her mouth. She'd never really understood the appeal of going down on a guy before, but with Smith, it all made perfect sense. She lost herself in the pleasure—both her own, and that of watching him find his. She bobbed her head, sucking harder.

"Come here, babe."

Her mouth slid off his cock, and she licked him once more. With a groan, he slid his hands beneath her underarms, and pulled her up and to the side.

For a moment, she thought that her fun was over, but

he spun her hips toward him, so that she was facing his cock. Then he pulled her knees over to straddle his face, so she was crouched over him. She let out a little squeak.

Oh. His mouth nudged between her legs, his beard rasping against her skin. She squirmed. *Oh, God.* Then he licked her.

She cried out, and then Smith smacked one palm against her ass.

"Back to work, sunshine."

She moved instantly, sucking his cock back into her mouth. As she sucked and licked, his tongue delved inside her, making it darn hard to concentrate.

"Focus, Kinsey."

She raised her head, panting from the pleasure. "I can't."

But she kept stroking him and lowered her head again, sucking him deep.

Smith returned the favor, and sucked her clit into his mouth. It was too much. She came instantly, screaming his name.

The next thing she knew, she was flat on the bed on her belly. His big weight behind her.

He drove his cock inside her and they both moaned.

Her pleasure was still vibrating through her as he thrust inside her. *God. So good.*

"It's so fucking good sliding inside you." His voice was like gravel. "I could stay right here, lodged deep, and be happy."

Her hands twisted in the covers. "Smith."

His thrusts increased in pace, his big body covering hers. She loved feeling the weight of him on top of her.

His hands circled her waist and he pulled her up on her knees.

"Fuck...Kinsey." He pulled her back onto his cock.

"Yes." She rocked back, meeting his thrusts.

With a blinding rush, Kinsey came again. Her cries weren't even coherent. With one last hard thrust, Smith drove deep, and groaned through his release.

Kinsey fell forward onto the bed. She was wrecked, in the best possible way. Smith pressed his hands to the bed on either side of her head, then he leaned down, kissing the back of her neck.

"Love the way you light up for me." His beard and lips brushed between her shoulder blades.

She turned her head to look back over her shoulder, languid and relaxed.

His hands moved over her back, stroking down her spine. "Every time I touch you, you're so damn hungry for me."

Kinsey felt heat in her cheeks. Was that a bad thing?

One of his hands slid between her legs, and she instantly opened for him. He cupped her.

"So wet. All for me."

When she looked into his face, she saw the possessive hunger on his features. There was clear satisfaction in his voice.

"And you like that?" she asked.

"Yeah." He leaned down and kissed her. "Best I've ever had, sunshine."

Now heat bloomed inside her, and it had nothing to do with embarrassment.

KINSEY LEANED FORWARD, staring into the mirror in the bathroom as she snipped at her hair. She tidied up the ends a little. She'd still need to visit a hairdresser, but for now, it wouldn't look like she'd had her hair cut by a toddler...or a terrorist bitch.

As she shifted, she felt a throb between her legs. A very pleasant reminder of what she'd spent the night doing. She looked at her eyes in the mirror, then she smiled.

The bathroom door opened, and a bare-chest Smith entered.

Her pulse spiked. "Hey."

His gaze moved straight to her hair, his eyes darkening.

She swallowed. "Does it look okay?"

"I'm sorry they did that, Kinsey. I'm sorry I let them take you."

She straightened. "You aren't to blame, big guy. Hell, Axel took a bullet trying to stop it." She tugged on the strands self-consciously. He'd made it clear he liked her hair and now he seemed pretty upset it was mostly gone.

A big hand slid into her shorter locks, cupping the side of her head. "You could shave it all off and you'd still be beautiful."

She smiled.

"It's cute. Suits you." He feathered her hair between his fingers.

"If my mama saw it, she'd be horrified. She hated short hair on a woman. She'd tell me I looked like a boy."

"You couldn't look like a boy if you tried." He paused, his gaze meeting hers in the mirror. "Home wasn't good?"

Kinsey sighed. "Home was a trailer in Sugarview, Tennessee. My daddy was a drunk and my mama was bitter about everything." Kinsey looked away. "When my father drank too much…"

Smith's hand tightened in her hair. "He hit you."

"I got good at ducking. And when I got older, I got good at reading the signs that a drunken rage was coming."

Smith cursed. "And your mother didn't step in?"

Kinsey let out a laugh. "No way. She was more than happy if he got distracted by me and saved her a slap."

"Bitch."

"Yes. And when I got older…I think she saw me as competition."

Smith pulled her closer. "Your beauty and goodness, I bet she couldn't stand it." He scowled. "I'd like to teach them both a lesson…"

Kinsey's heart melted. Her big, overprotective mountain man. "I escaped, Smith. I left them behind a long time ago and have no desire to look back."

He grunted.

"Now I live the life I want, filled with pretty things and a good job." She stroked his beard-covered jaw. God, he was so beautiful. "And now I have a handsome, strong man in my bed. Living the good life is the best revenge."

A look crossed his face and she tilted her head.

"What?"

He released a breath. "You. You escaped a shit situation and used it as motivation to make your life better."

He rubbed his thumb across her jaw. "I absorbed the shit and let it stay inside."

Her happiness drained away. "Smith—"

"Was married when I was young and dumb. Lila taught me some pretty bad lessons on relationships. Rubbed those wounds in so deep, I decided not to risk it again."

Kinsey swallowed. "Did you love her?"

He made a scoffing sound. "At the time, I thought I did. Once I got older and wiser, I realized I was thinking with my dick. Was glad I divorced her ass and joined the Navy."

Until that had gone bad as well.

"Then you lost your leg," Kinsey said quietly.

"Lost friends. Good men who should have come home to their families."

His brow was creased and she rubbed the groove. "I heard you saved a teammate, even with an injured foot."

Smith lifted a shoulder. "Gary made it. He's married, got two kids. Calls me every now and then."

"You did a hard job, a tough job that not many people can do. You saved lives and fought for our freedom." She went up on her toes. "You're my hero, Smith Creed."

"And you, with your smiles, and your candles, and the way you look for the good in everything, are mine."

She bit her lip. "Hey, don't make me cry." She pulled his head down and kissed him. "All my life, I wanted good things and never got them, you had good things and lost them. But I think our bad times are over, Smith."

"You are fucking sunshine in the darkness, Kinsey."

Oh, she loved that. She kissed him again and found

herself pushed up against the vanity. The kiss went on forever, then he lifted his head.

"I want to take you back to bed, but we're due to meet the others."

Kinsey pulled in a calming breath. "Okay."

"I think there are lots of good things ahead for us, sunshine, but first, we have some Mafia terrorists to deal with." He touched her hair, smoothing it behind her ear.

"Then let's go kick some bad guy ass."

WITH HIS ARM around Kinsey's shoulders, Smith walked into the computer room.

No surprise, there were wide grins all round. Smith stifled a sigh.

Axel was there, still looking a little white-faced. Kinsey broke away and hurried over to him.

He held up a hand. "I'm fine. No more hugging or nagging."

Kinsey ignored him and threw her arms around him.

With a disgruntled sigh, Axel hugged her back. "Enough. I had far worse injuries when I was in the fucking Army." He shot a glare at Nat, who was perched on a stool, her legs crossed, despite her fitted skirt. "And I never had to suffer through people nagging me into bed, nagging me to eat, and fussing all the damn time."

Nat sniffed, looking unconcerned. "You were shot, beaten, and had a concussion, Diaz."

"I. Am. Fine."

Nat nodded. "Because we'll make sure of it."

Blair coughed, but Smith was pretty certain she was fighting not to laugh.

"How are you doing, Kinsey?" Lachlan asked.

"She's glowing," Blair said. "So, I'd say she's feeling pretty good."

"Getting laid does that." Axel winked.

From beside Axel, Seth shook his head and looked at his boots. "Glad someone else is copping it for a change."

Kinsey's cheeks went pink and Smith scowled at his team.

Callie reached out and touched Kinsey's chin. "The bruising is looking better."

"I'm feeling good." She returned to Smith's side.

"I bet," Blair said.

Brooks stepped forward, tablet in hand. Today, his shirt said "I'm not the droid you're looking for." He was desperately trying to keep a straight face, and failing miserably. "If you guys are finished discussing Smith and Kinsey's sex life...?"

With a quiet groan, Kinsey pressed her face into Smith's chest.

"I can give you a bit longer if you need it," Brooks said.

Lachlan shook his head. "Let's get to work."

Brooks nodded, and the screens on the wall filled with images of men and women. "These are all the people who are known members of Cosca Unita."

The vibe in the room changed, everyone turning serious. Some of the pictures were surveillance shots, but others were mugshots. Clearly, these guys were no strangers to breaking the law.

"Oh, God," Kinsey murmured.

"The group is pretty well-funded," Brooks said. "But up until now, they haven't committed any high-profile attacks. It appears they are stepping up their game."

Suddenly, there was a ping from Brooks' tablet. He glanced at it and frowned.

"Brooks?" Lachlan prompted.

"Something's happening." Brooks frantically tapped the screen. "Oh, fuck. They're using the artifact."

Screens on the front wall filled with news broadcasts and social media sites, where people were sharing online videos from their phones.

Smith's gut hardened. He instantly recognized the Denver skyline and the mountains behind it.

Brooks turned on the sound.

An excited female newsreader leaned forward. "—vibrations. The entire building is shaking! We're going to our man, David, who is live on the scene."

A male reporter stood on a sidewalk, people running past him screaming and shouting.

"The building in question is the partially constructed Verge Tower."

The camera panned, and they had a perfect view of the half-built building. It was covered in scaffolding. It was also shaking, like it was in an earthquake. But no other buildings were moving.

"We've had reports that all the workers are clear of the building," the reporter said. "But that is unconfirmed at this stage."

"My God," Kinsey said, horrified.

Everyone in the room had their eyes glued to the

screen. More screams echoed from behind the reporter, followed by sirens.

The reporter turned, throwing out an arm. "No one can explain what the cause of the vibration is. Perhaps subsidence beneath the building, or some sort of gas explosion."

The screams increased in volume and the reporter gasped.

The building rumbled, as the top half of the structure broke loose from its foundations, rising up in the air.

Smith's chest locked as he watched the awesome display of power.

"Oh, my God," the reporter breathed, his mouth dropping open. "Jeff, are you getting this?"

Chunks of concrete crashed to the ground.

"Holy crap," Blair said.

"Unfucking believable," Axel ground out.

Smith pulled Kinsey closer, watching in horror as the building rose higher and higher. More pieces of masonry crashed down, broken loose by the building's vibrations. One large piece slammed into a car, leaving the vehicle a twisted wreck.

"They're using it," Kinsey whispered.

Smith wrapped his arms tightly around her.

They all watched as the skyscraper moved through the air.

"There are reports of some strange sound vibrations," the reporter said. "We're switching the view to our eye in the sky."

The image changed to video feed coming from a helicopter.

Everyone in the computer room watched as the building sailed through the air, perfectly controlled, and then moved over to hover above the Platte River.

All of a sudden, it crashed downward, hitting the water with a splash.

The room instantly filled with curses and angry muttering.

"They're testing its capabilities," Lachlan said, voice tight.

"Why Denver?" Nat asked.

They all looked at each other.

"Cosca Unita wants anarchy," Brooks said. "They want to bring the government down."

Smith's jaw clenched. "Buckley Air Force Base."

Lachlan and Seth cursed.

"Why's that so important?" Kinsey said.

"Buckley's home to the Space Based Infrared System," Smith said. "Has giant domes that house satellite dishes to pick up all infrared energy released around the planet. It's a missile detection and defense system."

"*The* missile detection system," Lachlan added.

"Air Force Academy near Colorado Springs," Callie added.

Fuck. Another thought occurred to Smith. "NORAD. The North American Aerospace Defense Command is also down at Colorado Springs. At Peterson Air Force Base."

Lachlan's face hardened. "Everyone prep. We're going to Denver."

CHAPTER THIRTEEN

Kinsey sat on Smith's bunk, watching him shove things in a big, black duffel bag.

Her stomach felt sick. People were hurt in Denver, and she knew this was just the beginning.

And it was all her damn fault.

She'd been here, enjoying the hell out of Smith, and meanwhile, Cosca Unita had been planning to kill and destroy.

"Sunshine." Smith sat on the bed beside her, one long finger moving beneath her chin. He tipped her face up.

"Smith, it's partly my fault—"

"We already talked about this."

"People are hurt. And we both know it's only going to get worse."

He pulled her close, and she knew that he wanted to shield her. She breathed in the scent of him, absorbing his strength.

"I'm going to stop them." His voice held a dark edge.

Her fingers dug into his arms. "That just freaks me out more." The last thing she wanted was for him to get hurt. "Now, I'll just worry about you and the others. That you'll get hurt like Axel did." She thought of Axel hurt—unconscious and bleeding—and she shuddered.

"Axel's fine. The man's got a damn hard head. Besides, this is our job." Smith ran his fingers through her hair. "This is what we do, and we're good at it."

Kinsey nodded, trying to take comfort from that. He leaned forward to kiss her. Slow and steady, and so Smith.

God, he smelled good. Her hands flexed on his skin. He felt good. Made her feel good.

Suddenly, the ring of a cellphone broke the moment.

"That's mine." She scrambled across the bed and grabbed it off the nightstand. "Hello?"

"Kinsey."

She sucked in a breath. "Enzo, you—"

The phone was snatched away. "You do not call her." Smith looked like he was about to explode. He paused. "Fuck." The word shot through the room like a bullet.

Kinsey gripped her hands together, watching him carefully.

Smith set the phone down, pressing the button to put it on speaker.

"Look, I snuck away for a minute," Enzo said. "Don't have long. I...shit. They never fucking told me that they were going to do this."

"They're terrorists, Enzo," Kinsey said.

"My cousin got me involved. He convinced me they wanted to change things, help the little guy."

Kinsey made an angry noise. "They kidnapped me! Twice. You helped them. They beat me and shot my friend. What did I ever do to you?"

"I know. I know." His shaky breath came through the line. "I never meant for you to get hurt."

Smith growled.

"They have bigger plans," Enzo added.

She bit her lip and glanced at Smith. He smoothed a hand down her arm.

"What?" Smith demanded.

"No. I can't talk over the phone. And I'll only talk to Kinsey."

Smith growled.

"Meet me in City Park in Denver. At the boathouse on the lake."

"No," Smith bit out.

"Enzo!" Kinsey said.

The line disconnected.

"Fuck." Smith spun, kicked a chair, and sent it skidding across the room.

Kinsey turned, watching him. "Smith—"

A muscle ticked in his jaw.

"I have to come to Denver."

He pressed a hand to the back of his neck. "No."

"You heard Enzo, he'll only meet with me. We need all the intel we can get on Cosca Unita, and what they have planned."

"No."

Kinsey went up on her toes, pressing her hands to Smith's chest. "You know I need to come. You'll keep me safe. We'll find out where these guys are, and what they

151

have planned. The quicker we do it, the sooner we can stop them. It could save lives."

Smith released a breath. "Dammit."

Kinsey knew she had him. "I need to help, Smith. I want to help end this."

He kissed her again. This kiss was hard, angry, and needy.

He lifted his head, pressing his forehead against hers. "If you get hurt..."

"I won't."

"If you do, I'll tear the world apart to make them pay."

Her belly flip-flopped. No one had ever cared about her the way he did. "Smith."

He took a deep breath. "Get dressed, sunshine. And pack some things. We have a flight to catch and bad guys to stop."

SMITH STEPPED out of the rented SUV and glanced up at the renovated warehouse in front of them. They were in Denver's lower downtown district, known as LoDo. The warehouse looked like it had been home to some factory in a past life, but now, it housed the offices of Treasure Hunter Security.

The security outfit mainly provided protection for archeological digs, expeditions, and museum exhibits. The owners, and most of the people they employed, were former Navy SEALs. Smith didn't know them personally, but he'd heard good things.

They'd knocked up against Team 52 in the field a couple of times, but after some diplomatic conversation, they were now allies.

The glass door to the warehouse swung open, and two tall, wide-shouldered men stepped out. Smith eyed them and they looked back, faces set and expressionless.

It was obvious they were brothers. Declan and Callum Ward.

Another guy stepped out, no less tall or muscled, but he was wearing a suit. He waved them inside.

Smith looked at Lachlan, who nodded. He grabbed Kinsey's hand, and along with the team, headed toward the warehouse. Axel was with them. Despite a bullet wound, he'd refused to stay back at base.

Callie had yelled at him. Then Nat had yelled at him. But he'd dug his heels in.

"Can't go up against these guys one man down. The bullet didn't do too much damage and Callie can pump me with painkillers and stimulants."

Looking at him, you couldn't tell he'd been shot yesterday. Callie had a backpack full of drugs with her in case he needed them.

They entered the warehouse and passed a reception desk, boots echoing on the concrete floor.

"Good to see you, Lachlan." The man in the suit held out his hand.

Lachlan shook it. "You too, Alastair."

Special Agent Alastair Burke was head of the FBI's Art Crime Team. They'd worked with him a few times, most recently when they'd helped save him and his woman from the head of a black-market antiquities ring in Washington, DC.

"We're happy to help," Burke added.

From beside him, Dec Ward nodded. "Especially after DC."

Cal crossed his arms over his chest. "And especially when some fuckers are tearing our city up."

The click of high heels echoed through the space, and a woman pushed forward into the group. "Don't just leave them standing there, invite them in." The woman had glossy, dark hair that brushed her jaw. She wore dark jeans with a bright-red shirt. She also had Declan Ward's eyes. Smith knew this was Darcy Ward —Dec and Cal's sister, and Burke's woman. She was also co-owner of Treasure Hunter Security with her brothers.

They all moved inside, heading over to a long conference table. There were more tough-looking people standing around, along with a few women.

Darcy waved a hand. "THS badasses meet the Team 52 badasses."

There were narrowed looks, chin lifts, and a few smiles.

Darcy grabbed a small metal case and set it on the table. She flipped it open. "Here's the tracker you requested. It's undetectable."

This was the plan Lachlan and Brooks had cooked up. Get Enzo to place an undetectable tracker on the artifact.

"Completely undetectable?" Smith asked.

Darcy nodded. "It's transparent, won't show up on

scanners. We used it in DC. The range is somewhat limited..."

"Our guy can improve on that," Lachlan said.

Darcy's blue-gray gaze narrowed. "Then I hope you share that with us. You know, another show of good faith."

Lachlan lifted his chin.

Darcy closed the box and handed it to Lachlan. "Good luck. Shut these bastards down."

"Thanks. This'll help." Lachlan handed the case to Blair.

"I'm still pissed about Africa." A handsome man with dark skin and dark hair folded his muscular arms over his chest.

Beside him, a slim, blonde woman in a pantsuit jabbed an elbow in his side. "Let it go, Hale."

Smith scowled. A Team 52 drone had opened fire on the pair—Hale Carter and Special Agent Elin Alexander —on a mission in Africa. Team 52 hadn't known that the couple were undercover at the time. His team didn't like making mistakes.

"It was a mistake," Lachlan said.

"And we regret it," Smith added.

Kinsey leaned into him.

"Take it as a compliment that we had no fucking clue that you guys were on that mission." Smith lifted his chin. "You guys are good." He met Hale's dark gaze. "As a former SEAL, I'm not surprised."

Hale's face lost some of its hard edge. "Well, when you put it like that..."

Elin smiled.

"I just don't like remembering my woman under fire," Hale continued.

Smith lifted his chin. "Know the feeling."

Hale's gaze moved to Kinsey, lingering on the last of her fading bruises. Sympathy flickered in his eyes.

"We're pretty damn concerned about what happened downtown," Dec said.

A hush fell over the room.

"These terrorists are dangerous," Lachlan said. "And they have a dangerous weapon. We'll stop them. It's our job." His gaze moved to Hale. "And despite Africa, which I am sorry happened, we're very good at it."

Dec nodded. "You guys saved our asses in Antarctica."

"And DC," Darcy added, glancing at Burke.

"We'll find these bastards and close them down," Smith said.

"If you need any assistance, we'll be on standby." Dec nodded at Lachlan. "You need help, just say the word."

Team 52 said their goodbyes, and soon they were striding back to the two black rental SUVs Kinsey had organized for them at the airport.

Smith glanced at his watch. "We need to meet Enzo in twenty minutes."

Kinsey set her shoulders back and nodded.

City Park wasn't far away. After a short drive, they parked in front of the Denver Museum of Nature and Science, which sat in one corner of the park.

From the museum, lush, green grass and trees ran down toward a lake, and the historic boat pavilion built on the edge of it. The elegant cream structure was built in a Spanish-style, with lots of towers and arches. The city skyline lay in the distance, and behind that the mountains.

"Wow, that's some view," Kinsey said.

"We'll come back. Spend a few days here, then head up into the mountains to meet my parents."

Her blue eyes went wide. "Meet your parents."

"You need this." Smith held out the small box with the tracker in it.

She nodded, her fingers wrapping around it.

"You'll also need this." He held up a tiny microdot earpiece. He pushed her now-short hair behind her ear, and slid the small device in place. "We'll be close by."

She smiled. "I know."

"Anything worries you, anything at all, you run."

She nodded, a look of determination in her eye.

"You see a weapon, you say the codeword."

She blinked. "What codeword?"

"Pick one."

She tapped her lips. "Thor."

Smith scowled. "Thor?"

She shrugged. "A good-looking god of thunder and lightning. What's not to like?"

His scowl deepened. "He wears a lame cape, right?"

Kinsey smiled, leaning in and pressing her hands to his chest. "I like him because he's got a beard. He's got blond hair and a muscular bod. You've got a rougher, more rugged thing going on, but he makes me think of you."

Smith shook his head and jerked her up for a kiss. "Go. Be careful."

She smiled, then turned, heading toward the pavilion. *His.* That one word reverberated in his head.

The rest of his team dissolved into the surrounding trees and grassy area. Not far away, Blair reclined on the grass like she was worshipping the sun. Lachlan and Seth weren't anywhere in sight. Callie was sitting on a bench, looking like she was enjoying the view. Axel was chatting with a female jogger.

Smith found a place close to the pavilion. Not as close as he'd like. He stood under the shade of a tree, and watched Kinsey walk onto the small, covered deck that protruded out over the lake. She leaned against the railing, fidgeting.

He touched his ear. "Relax."

"You relax," she snapped.

"Don't talk."

She poked her tongue out at the lake. It looked like she was doing it to the ducks.

Smith shook his head. So damn cute.

"Incoming." Lachlan's murmur came across the line.

Smith spotted the dickhead heading straight toward Kinsey. Enzo's movements were jerky and nervous, and he continually glanced around the park.

"Kinse—" The man's voice came clearly across the line.

"That's close enough, Enzo," she said.

"I...I'm sorry."

She remained silent.

"I want to help," he continued. "It's gone too far. I never wanted you to get hurt, and I sure as hell don't want to be a mass murderer."

"Where is the artifact?"

"They've got it in a truck. They're about to move it."

"Where?" Kinsey asked.

"Into the mountains." Enzo fidgeted. "Fuck, Kinsey, they're going to attack NORAD."

Shit. Smith had guessed it, but he still didn't like having it confirmed. He saw Kinsey reach into her pocket and hold up the small case. "There is a tracker in here—"

Enzo raised his hands. "No—"

"You want to help?" Kinsey said. "It's time to man up. Before more people are hurt or killed."

The man dragged in a long, shaky breath, then he nodded. He took the case.

"The tracker is undetectable," Kinsey assured him. "Get it on the artifact. The team I work with will take it from there."

Enzo gave her a nervous nod, then shoved his longish hair off his face. "I'm sorry about everything, Kinsey."

She sighed. "Me, too."

"Maybe after this is all over—" The man's voice had a hopeful edge.

Smith growled and straightened.

"Nope," Kinsey said. "I've got a man."

Enzo's eyebrows rose. "You do?"

"He's big and strong, and he fights to help people, not hurt them."

Enzo's shoulders sagged. "Right."

"Plant the tracker, Enzo."

The man gave her another nod, then spun on his boots, and walked away.

A moment later, Smith saw Kinsey crossing the grass toward him.

Her gaze met his. "NORAD."

"I know."

Smith wrapped his arms around her. "You did a great job, sunshine."

"Maybe I'll apply for a spot on the team," she said with a grin.

He scowled at her. "Hell, no."

CHAPTER FOURTEEN

K insey sat in the back of the SUV, watching the trees slide past. They were heading up into the mountains west of Colorado Springs, and if she wasn't so nervous and upset, she'd probably appreciate the gorgeous views.

Team 52 all sat around her, checking their weapons.

Her phone vibrated in her hand and she lifted it to her ear. "Kinsey Beck."

The man she'd spoken with about organizing snow-mobiles for the team was on the other end. As the man talked, she nodded. "Okay, yes. I need six of them. Great, I'll transfer payment. Thanks so much."

Smith glanced at her. "Good?"

"Good. The snowmobiles are sorted and will be waiting for us."

The weather in Denver had been sunny and pleasant, but here in the mountains, while there was still blue sky, there was snow on the ground.

Kinsey fiddled with the vest Smith had given her. Team 52 were wearing civilian winter gear, but she knew they all had bullet-proof vests on.

It appeared Enzo had successfully placed the tracker. She arched her head, looking at the screen on the dash of the vehicle. She saw the glowing dot they were heading toward.

They were heading to Cheyenne Mountain, just west of Colorado Springs. While NORAD's main operations were now run out of the nearby Peterson Air Force Base, the bunker at the Cheyenne Mountain Complex housed some of NORAD's critical systems, and was the alternate, back up location. It appeared Cosca Unita were going to attack the mountain first, and then probably the Air Force base.

"Okay, listen up." Lachlan turned around in the front seat. "We go in as we planned. We move in on the snowmobiles and follow the tracker to their location. We stop Cosca Unita from using the artifact, no matter what. Got it?"

There were rumbles of agreement from the team.

Kinsey swallowed. She was well aware it wouldn't be that simple.

God, if Cosca Unita did use it...

Kinsey knew that Cheyenne Mountain was designed to withstand a nuclear attack. But could it withstand an ancient Tibetan artifact that could possibly rip the mountain on top of it apart, stone by stone?

She blew out a breath. Damn, it was hard having the weight of the world on your shoulders. And she knew Team 52 did this every time they went on a mission.

After this was over, she planned to curl up in bed and sleep for a week. Preferably with Smith.

She glanced at him, taking in his rugged face and that dark beard. She felt a niggle of uncertainty.

After this was over, she wouldn't need saving or rescuing or protecting. Once she was safe, he was going to realize that she was just boring, old Kinsey.

She pulled in a breath. This wasn't the time to worry about her love life. They had to save the world first.

Blair had turned off the highway, and they were heading down a narrow, empty road. Ahead, a huge truck and trailer were parked on the shoulder. When they stepped out, she saw the snowmobile guy looked exactly how he sounded on the phone. He was a grizzled, old man in the typical mountain man uniform: jeans, boots, and a flannel shirt.

Kinsey raised a hand. "Hi. Are you Shep?"

"Yeah."

The team inspected the snowmobiles and pulled them off the trailers.

"The lady said you're up here for a weekend to explore," Shep said.

No one answered the unasked question.

"Not that much interesting around here." Shep shrugged. "Only a bunch of antennae and transmitters on top of the mountain, for radio, television, and cellphones."

Kinsey smiled. "We'll, um, just enjoy the scenery." She tilted her head. "So, nothing else worth looking at?"

Shep shrugged. "Only other thing is the abandoned Little Mollie mine."

Kinsey felt everyone go tense. "What's that?" She kept her voice conversational.

"Old gold mine. Opened back in the 1870s. Never got much out of it." His gaze narrowed on Kinsey. "I'd steer clear. Old tunnels are dangerous."

She smiled. "Fascinating. We're more just here for the sport and natural beauty, but we might check it out."

Shep looked at her smile and blinked a few times. "Right. Take care."

Kinsey thanked the man again and watched him drive away. When she turned back, the team had the snowmobiles prepped and ready to leave.

Smith stepped in front of her. "Kinsey, maybe you should stay here with the SUV—"

Her heart sank.

"And if the Cosca Unita find her?" Blair asked. "All alone? Unprotected?"

Smith glared at his friend.

"She's safer with us," Lachlan said.

Smith's jaw went tight and he reached back, pulling out a large handgun from the storage on the snowmobile. He handed it to her. "You know how to use this?"

She did. When she'd joined the team, they'd made her practice at the range. She didn't love guns, but she kept up her skills. She nodded.

"Show me."

She checked it over. "Decocker." She touched the lever. Next, she dumped the magazine, checked it, and shoved it back into the gun.

He nodded. "Keep it on you."

Finally, everyone turned to the snowmobiles and mounted up.

Smith climbed on and looked at her. "You ride with me. If I give you an order, you obey. I tell you to run, you run. Got it?"

"Got it." The word obey wasn't one she loved, but Smith and the others were the experts in this situation.

She climbed on behind him. She'd never been on a snowmobile before. He handed her a set of goggles and a helmet. She pulled them on, then wrapped her arms around Smith, and a second later he started the engine. The snowmobile vibrated beneath her.

Lachlan zipped off, Blair following. Then, Smith gunned the engine and they took off.

Oh, boy. They darted through the trees, gliding over the snow.

She knew this was a dangerous mission, and there was a lot at stake, but this was fun. She held on tight to Smith and let herself enjoy the ride.

SMITH FOLLOWED the rest of his team, enjoying the feel of the snowmobile under his control. It had been a while since he'd visited his dad and taken his snowmobile out.

He dodged around some large trees, Kinsey's hold tightening on him. He liked the feel of her, her warmth tucked up against his back.

Not that he wanted her on this mission.

He wanted her safe, not headed into potential danger.

He muttered a curse. He had to focus on getting the mission done. Take out Cosca Unita and recover the artifact. Then Kinsey would be safe and secure.

They all knew that it was likely Cosca Unita was using this mine as a hideout. The tracker was leading right in that direction, and that was the first location they were going to investigate.

Ahead, Lachlan slowed his snowmobile. He glanced back and even through the goggles, his gaze caught Smith's. Smith nodded. He knew his leader wanted him to take the lead and look for signs of any tracks.

Smith moved into the lead, taking in the landscape around them.

He pulled in a deep breath of fresh air. The mountains were in his veins, but he had to admit that his cabin in Vegas, and the vast, empty beauty of the desert, called to him now as well.

Although nothing quite matched the way the woman sitting behind him called to him. The way he needed her in his arms. The way she soothed him and made him happy.

Moving over a large mound of snow, his snowmobile went airborne. As they landed, he heard Kinsey's sweet, excited laugh. Maybe he'd bring her here for Christmas. He'd find a nice cabin, make love to her in front of the fire.

Suddenly, Smith spotted something ahead and slowed. He pulled the snowmobile to a stop.

He heard the others pull in behind him, and when

Kinsey scooted back, he swung off the machine to check the churned-up snow he'd spotted.

He shoved his goggles up and crouched. He saw the trail leading into the trees.

"Tracks," he said. "Boots and snowmobiles."

Lachlan lifted his head, scanning the trees. "We're close. They're here."

Smith nodded.

"Let's keep moving," Lachlan said.

"We'll probably have to abandon the snowmobiles soon and go in on foot. Otherwise, they'll hear us coming."

Soon, they were all back on the snowmobiles, following the trail.

"We're getting close to the mine," Kinsey said in his ear.

All of a sudden, gunfire broke out. Bullets hit the trees closest to them, tearing up the branches and bark.

Fuck. Smith swerved. A branch hit him in the face and he ignored it. He gunned the machine, heard more gunfire.

Behind him, he heard the whine of engines, and knew the others were evading the bullets.

Smith had to protect Kinsey. He felt her hands gripping his waist.

Then Smith heard CXMs firing. Some of his team were returning fire.

"Team 52." Brooks' voice came through Smith's earpiece. "You have snowmobiles incoming. A lot of them."

Of course, they did. Smith pulled out his SIG, firing

one handed, while he tried to steer the snowmobile. Two snowmobiles, topped by men in black winter gear, came close and he fired on them.

"Hold on," he shouted back at Kinsey.

He aimed for some trees, racing through a narrow gap. Branches hit at them. He saw a mound of snow ahead and sped up. They hit it, went airborne.

They landed, and when Smith turned the snowmobile, he got a clear view of Lachlan, standing up on his machine, shooting back at the incoming fighters behind them.

All of a sudden, the roar of an engine made Smith jerk his head around.

"Smith! Watch out!" Kinsey screamed.

A snowmobile shot out of the trees right beside him.

Fuck.

They almost collided, but Smith revved the snowmobile and swerved to the right. The Cosca Unita rider was right beside them. He raised a handgun, aiming right at Smith.

Bang.

When the rider tumbled off into the snow, his snowmobile flew forward, out of control, and slammed into a tree. Smith swerved again and glanced back. Kinsey was holding the SIG he'd given her.

He smiled. That was his girl.

More gunfire, and Smith jerked the snowmobile to the left. They hit a rock and it sent a huge jolt through the machine.

Dammit. Smith fought to keep them from tipping over.

And that's when he felt Kinsey fly off the back.

No.

Smith pulled on the brakes, skidding. Snow flew up around the snowmobile. He turned, aiming to head straight back to her.

She was up on her knees, firing her weapon.

Smith turned his head and his gut clenched. Another Cosca Unita snowmobile was gunning right at her. The bastard was going to run her over.

Smith accelerated. He *had* to get to her.

Suddenly, a body dropped from a tree above, knocking Smith off his snowmobile.

He landed flat on his back, snow flying everywhere. He caught a glimpse of his snowmobile crashing through some trees before coming to an abrupt stop.

Rolling, he turned and saw another Cosca Unita fighter. The man rose. He was a big bastard, even a few inches taller than Smith. He had a bald head, and a snake tattoo slithering up the side of his neck. A brawler.

Dammit. Smith didn't have time for this. He had to get to Kinsey.

The Cosca Unita soldier grinned at Smith, sunlight glinting off a gold tooth.

Smith braced, and the man rushed him like a linebacker.

CHAPTER FIFTEEN

—————————

Heart pounding, Kinsey watched the Cosca Unita man in snow gear riding his snowmobile straight at her.

Shit. Anger burst through her. She raised her gun and started firing.

She peppered his snowmobile with bullets, and the machine skidded to the side. The man flew off, sailing through the air.

Kinsey spun and started running through the snow. But it was too deep for her to move quickly, and she felt like she was running through molasses.

A weight hit her, tackling her to the ground. She got a face full of snow and her gun flew out of her hand.

She shoved the person off of her, and raised up on her hands and knees. As she lifted her head, she caught a quick glimpse of the rest of Team 52. They were all fighting with the attackers.

And she knew that they'd keep fighting, they'd never give up.

Nor would she.

She scrambled for her gun, the butt of it sticking out of the snow not far away.

"Nuh-uh." The Cosca Unita man gripped her ankle, and dragged her back through the snow on her belly. "You're my leverage."

She struggled against him, but he was too big and strong. She kicked, catching him in the chest. He grunted, but didn't let her go. He rose, yanked her roughly to her feet, and started dragging her into the trees.

"You'll get these bastards to back off," he said.

"They'll never back off. It's their job to stop terrorists like you."

The man scowled. "We'll see."

He kept pulling her farther away from the others, and Kinsey struggled, fighting him every step of the way. She knew Team 52 would come for her. Smith would come.

They moved across some rocky ground and she yanked hard, breaking free. With a curse, the man turned and she kicked him. Right between the legs.

He made a terrible sound and doubled over.

Kinsey took off running. Branches slapped at her arms and face, but she kept going. The snow was deep and she sank to her knees in spots, but she kept moving.

She finally had a man she loved, and she wasn't going to let Cosca Unita and this asshole screw that up.

Her boots slipped and she went down on her butt. Hard. *Ow.* She leaped back up and kept going. The sounds of pursuit came from behind her and her pulse spiked.

The man was clearly still coming after her.

"Kinsey." Smith's voice in her ear.

"I'm here."

"You okay?"

She sucked air into her burning lungs. "Running from a bad guy."

Smith cursed. "Where are you?"

Oh, God. She looked around. She had no idea. "I don't know. In the trees."

"Hold tight, babe. I'm coming."

"Hurry."

A moment later, she broke out of the trees. But instead of the clearing where she'd last seen Team 52, she was right at the edge of a steep cliff.

Oh, God. She skidded to a stop, windmilling her arms.

The sound of a body crashing through the trees echoed behind her, her attacker almost colliding with her. He grabbed her arm, fingers biting into her bicep.

Movement at the base of the cliff caught Kinsey's gaze. Down below, men in black winter gear were moving in and out of an old mine entrance cut into the side of the hill. A rusted metal structure sat higher up the slope, skeletal against the sky, and she knew it had to have been part of the old gold mine.

Suddenly, the man beside her jerked backward.

His violent move sent Kinsey stumbling. She landed on her hands and knees. She swiveled, ready to blast him, when she realized what had happened.

Smith had happened.

She watched him grab the man and throw him to the ground. Before the man could get back up, Smith was on him, punching him with hard, steady, brutal hits.

She winced.

"Kinsey?"

She looked up at Callie. The medic held out a hand and helped Kinsey up.

The rest of Team 52 stood nearby, watching Smith impassively. The man who had taken Kinsey was now collapsed on the snowy ground, bloodied and groaning.

"Smith," Kinsey said.

His head shot up.

"Enough," she murmured. "I'm okay."

Smith rose, pulling the man up with him. Then he tossed the man aside. As Axel and Seth moved to fully subdue the Cosca Unita fighter, Smith strode toward Kinsey.

One look into that face she loved, and she saw he was on the edge of losing his control. He also had a cut on his face, and she reached up and stroked it.

"I'm right here, baby," she murmured.

His arms shot out, wrapping around her and pulling her so close to him that her toes left the ground.

"I'm here," she said. "I'm okay."

Smith pressed his face to her hair, and she felt his big body tremble. She ran her hand through his hair and then finally, he relaxed.

Crisis averted. She leaned into him.

Lachlan stepped forward. "Time to shut these fuckers down."

Smith raised his head and nodded. Together, all of

them lined up along the cliff, looking down at the activity below.

"Let's end this," Smith said.

SMITH CROUCHED BEHIND SOME ROCKS, studying the mine entrance. The rest of the team was dotted behind other clusters of rocks and trees nearby. They'd trekked down the hillside, and now were only forty feet away from the mine entrance.

Cosca Unita had several trucks pulled up out front, and were busy loading supplies into them.

"They're getting ready to move out," Smith murmured.

Getting ready to attack Cheyenne Mountain and NORAD.

"You see the artifact anywhere?" Lachlan asked.

Smith shook his head. "Nope."

"Time to find it."

Smith glanced down. Kinsey was right beside him, peering around the rock. "You stay back here, out of sight."

She nodded, touching his arm. "Be safe. All of you."

He pulled her in for a fast, hard kiss. Then he spun, moving with the rest of his team as they crept forward.

They ducked from tree to rock to tree, staying in cover. Once they were closer to the mine entrance, Smith and Axel pulled some smoke grenades off their belts.

Axel looked at him and nodded. They lobbed the grenades, and they landed right near the trucks.

Bang. Bang.

There were shouts and confusion. The smoke rose in a cloud. Smith heard gunfire.

Team 52 rose, CXMs lifted, and moved in.

Additional fighters ran through the smoke, and Smith fired. *Bam.* Swiveled. *Bam. Bam.*

Ahead, he watched Lachlan kick one man, and aim his CXM at another soldier's chest.

"Where's the artifact?" Lachlan's voice was ice-cold.

"Fuck you!"

Lachlan swiveled the CXM and slammed the butt into the man's face, knocking him out. "Wrong answer."

Through the smoke, Smith spotted two men running to a canvas-covered, bulky pile of supplies.

That could be the artifact. "Lachlan, I have eyes on—"

But when the men yanked the canvas sheet off, what he saw made his blood run cold.

"Turret!" he shouted.

Smith dived, just as a rapid-fire hail of machine-gun fire sprayed all around them.

His team was cursing in his earpiece. They all took cover where they could—behind stacks of crates and the trucks. More deadly waves of bullets pinged all around them, tearing up the ground.

"What now?" Blair barked on the comm line.

Seth popped up and fired, but a hail of bullets came back at him, and he dropped back. They were all pinned down.

Dammit. Smith glanced at their surroundings, looking for a way out.

"Someone needs to circle around and shut down that turret," Lachlan bit out.

Smith eyed the nearby cliff. "I can sneak in along the base of the cliff, get in close, and neutralize the turret from the side."

"Too risky," Lachlan said. "You'll be in their line of fire. If they spot you..."

"Not if you guys make a big enough distraction."

From their hiding places nearby, Blair and Axel grinned.

"I'm good at distractions," Axel said.

Lachlan's gaze narrowed. "Okay, let's do it."

Every muscle in Smith's body was tense. He waited for his team to act, and a second later, several grenades rolled in close to the turret. CXMs opened fire.

Leaping up, Smith sprinted across the open ground.

Boom. Boom.

"This is better than the Fourth of July!" Axel shouted.

Bullets hit the dirt near Smith and he dodged, zigzagging as he ran. It was some asshole with an assault rifle.

"I've got him, Smith," Callie said.

The gunfire cut off. He ran in close to the rocks at the base of the cliff face, and slid in behind some large boulders. He pressed his back to the rock, lifted his CXM, and took a second to suck in some air.

Then he rose, circling in closer to the turret. He aimed for a stack of boxes.

A Cosca Unita soldier leaped out, popping up from behind the crates. *Fuck.* Smith changed direction. The man fired and Smith fired back. The Cosca Unita asshole leaped onto the boxes, aiming right at Smith.

Smith took his time, aimed, fired.

The man cried out and fell off the crates.

"Smith!" Lachlan's roar.

Smith turned his head...the turret was tracking in his direction.

Shit. He sprinted for the nearest cover, but it was too far. The universe seemed to be moving in slow motion. He wasn't going to make it.

Kinsey's smiling face filled his head.

Then he heard the sound of a gunning engine.

His head snapped up.

One of the Cosca Unita trucks was driving toward him, bouncing over the rough ground. Its tailgate was open and boxes were falling out of the back of it.

He saw Kinsey's pale face in the driver's seat.

What the hell?

She drove past him, right between him and the turret.

The machine gun opened fire, bullets ripping into the truck.

Kinsey. *No. Fuck, no!*

CHAPTER SIXTEEN

As bullets ripped into the truck, Kinsey ducked down below the dashboard, throwing her arms over her head.

Suddenly, a long, droning sound echoed outside the vehicle. *What the hell?* It was like the sound of a horn in some fantasy movie.

The truck jolted and she froze. She looked out the window and saw... *Oh, God.* The truck was lifting up *off the ground.*

Trying not to hyperventilate, she stared in shock. Outside the truck, several boulders were also rising up into the air, ripped out of the snow and dirt.

Shit, shit, shit. She quickly slid to the passenger side of the truck, peering out. This was not good. Not good. The truck was getting higher and higher in the air.

Then, one boulder dropped down. It rushed toward where Lachlan and Seth were standing.

Oh, God.

The men sprinted, diving out of the way. Another huge stone rocketed down, slamming into the ground, sending snow flying.

The truck kept rising, higher and higher.

She *had* to get out of this truck before it came crashing back to Earth too.

Kinsey opened the door, looking down. Wow, it was a long way to the ground.

Suddenly, the truck tilted a little, and she slid across the seat, heading for the open door. With a gasp, she frantically grabbed the door frame.

"Kinsey!"

She heard Smith's shout both in her ear and below her. She looked down. He was running right beneath the truck. Guns were still firing, but of course, he acted like he was bulletproof.

God, he was going to get shot.

"Jump!" he yelled.

Her insides clenched. It was a long drop. *Oh, shit.* She licked her lips.

Smith held his arms up. "Jump, sunshine. I'll catch you."

All she had to do was trust Smith. And she did. The man had never let her down.

Kinsey let go of the door and jumped.

She dropped fast, her heart in her throat.

Smith caught her, going down on one knee.

"Got you."

Then he was up and running. He slid them behind some rocks, and when Kinsey caught her breath, she noticed Callie nearby. The woman had her CXM up and was firing on the bad guys.

"You all right?" Smith's hands skimmed over Kinsey's arms.

She nodded and turned her head. *Jesus.* Rocks were hanging in the air, like gravity had disappeared.

Wow. It was as amazing as it was scary. The horn sound was still vibrating through the air, and above them on the hillside, more rocks were tearing loose from their resting places.

Lachlan sprinted in, leaping over a rock, and landing in a crouch. "We need to find the artifact and shut it down."

Smith nodded.

"Looks like the artifact doesn't levitate people," Lachlan said.

"Kinsey jumped out of the truck," Smith said. "Nothing held her up."

"Why?" she asked.

Lachlan shrugged. "I'll let Ty work that out."

Smith spun and cupped Kinsey's cheeks. "Stay here. And this time, *don't* move."

"Roger that."

"I mean it, Kinsey." There was a deep, unhappy groove in his forehead. "No more leaping into trucks and driving into a rain of bullets."

She lifted her chin. "To save you, I'd do it again, Smith Creed."

His scowl deepened. "Kinsey—"

She shook her head. "You risk yourself to save me all the time. I'm allowed to do it to save the man I—"

Her breath stuttered. *Love.* She loved him. This

wasn't just a serious attraction or crush. Kinsey loved this man. All the way through.

"The man you what?" His gaze was intense.

All of a sudden, a rock slammed into the ground nearby. The dirt beneath them shook, and snow sprayed over them like a wave.

Smith shook his head. "We'll discuss this later." He pressed a quick kiss to her mouth, then he rose.

Kinsey watched as Lachlan and Callie flanked him. The three of them raced into the fight, and Smith tossed a grenade.

Staying crouched behind the rock, Kinsey pulled in a deep breath. This would all be over soon.

A hand clamped down on her arm and she spun, expecting to see one of the team.

Instead, she looked up into Enzo's face.

"You have to come with me." He looked panicked, a crazed look in his eye.

She yanked her arm away. "No."

"Yes." He grabbed her jacket and yanked her up. "I'm trying to protect you."

She snorted. "Yeah, right."

"I love you, Kinsey."

Her eyebrows rose. "What?"

"I realized that I love you, and I need to protect you."

Fighting the urge to laugh hysterically, she yanked away from him, hard. "You're joking."

"You kept all my flowers."

She blinked. "I gave them away, Enzo. You're crazy."

His jaw hardened. "I'm not—"

"You don't know the first thing about love. Sorry,

Enzo, I'm in love with a mountain man badass. *He* protects me, or I damn well protect myself."

"No. You're mine. I loved you the minute I saw you. You're so beautiful."

Oh, God. She hadn't thought things could get any worse.

Enzo gripped her arm again, and this time he didn't let her pull free. They struggled for several moments, before he pulled her out of her hiding place and into the trees.

He gripped her chin and yanked her face up. Then he shoved a finger in her ear.

"Ow!"

He pressed hard and when he pulled his hand back, she saw her tiny microdot earpiece on his finger. He dropped it in the snow. Then he grabbed her hand and tugged her forward.

Kinsey kicked him. She hit his knee and he fell into the snow. She turned and ran.

But she didn't get far. Enzo tackled her and they rolled through the snow.

"Let me go!" She punched at his head.

His hands clamped on her arms and he subdued her. "I'm not letting you go." He pulled her up and dragged her back toward the trees.

"I regret the day I ever saw you," she spat.

"I'll take care of you and make you change your mind."

SMITH RAN, firing on the Cosca Unita fighters. Rocks slammed down all around him.

Fuck. He dived out of the way, rolled, and saw another rock heading right at him. He rolled again and leaped to his feet.

The rest of Team 52 were doing the same—firing, running, diving for cover.

"Anyone see the artifact?" Lachlan asked.

"No," Blair answered. She had her CXM raised, the front of her jacket splattered with mud.

Moving together, they spread out, firing on the last of the fighters.

Suddenly, the sound of the artifact cut off. They all froze.

Where the hell was it? Smith scanned around. There was no sign of it.

Then Smith heard the roar of a snowmobile. *Shit.* They all spun, just in time to see a man on a snowmobile riding off into the trees. A big, black box was lashed to the back of the machine.

"After him!" Lachlan ordered.

They sprinted back toward the hill where they'd hidden their snowmobiles. Smith rounded the rock where he'd left Kinsey.

His heart stopped. She wasn't there.

"Kinsey?" He pressed a finger to his earpiece. "Kinsey, where are you?"

No response.

"Shit." Lachlan spun, swinging his CXM onto his shoulder. "Brooks? Can you track Kinsey?"

A second later, Brooks voice came over the line. "Her

earpiece tracker is showing her just feet away from you guys."

"Well, she's not here," Lachlan said.

"Someone removed her fucking earpiece," Smith growled.

Lachlan's eyes flashed. "Callie, you stay with Smith. Find Kinsey. Blair, Seth, Axel, and I will intercept the artifact."

Lachlan and the others all sprinted up the hill toward their snowmobiles. Moments later, Smith heard them roar off.

"Whoever took her can't have gone far," Callie said.

Smith bent down, studying the ground. That's when he spotted the boot marks—one larger pair belonging to a man, and a smaller pair that had to be Kinsey's. He lifted his head. The trail led into the trees.

Someone had taken her.

Both pissed and worried, Smith rose. "Someone definitely grabbed her." His hands tightened on his rifle.

He jogged toward the trees, Callie falling in behind him as he followed the tracks. They climbed a hill and reached a clearing.

More tracks—different ones. "Fuck. They got on a snowmobile."

"Let's get our snowmobiles and follow them," Callie said. "Where are they headed?"

"Same direction as the others."

Callie nodded. "Toward Cheyenne Mountain."

They jogged back to the snowmobiles, and soon, Smith was flying through the trees, trying to keep his cool. If anyone had put another bruise on her...

"We'll get her back," Callie said in his earpiece. "She's smart, and she hasn't lost it through any of this. You chose a good woman, Smith."

He hadn't chosen. She'd been made for him. Smith blew out a breath. In his head, he saw Kinsey's smile, her glow, watched her rubbing Hercules' head. She was *his*. His sunshine, like a beam of pure light in the darkness.

Soon, they cleared the trees, and down below lay the entrance to Cheyenne Mountain. The portal in the side of the mountain was protected by a short length of steel tunnel, barbed-wire fences, and guards.

The mournful howl of the Tibetan artifact rang through the air once again.

Dammit. Ahead, at the heavily protected gate of the base, he watched a Humvee float up into the air. A siren sounded.

Then Smith heard gunfire. He traded a look with Callie. The gunfire was closer.

They crested a snow-covered hill, and he saw Lachlan and the others. They were firing on a small group of Cosca Unita fighters on the hillside.

But where the hell was Kinsey?

Bullets whizzed past and Smith ducked low over the handlebars.

"Incoming," Callie yelled.

A second group of Cosca Unita fighters broke out of the trees. These guys had to be a distraction. Protecting whoever was operating the artifact.

Down at the base's entrance, rocks, lengths of fence, and vehicles were floating into the sky. Then, in succession, they rained down, one by one.

Boom. Boom. Boom.

Guards ran in all directions.

More bullets, and Smith swung his CXM up, spraying fire on the Cosca Unita soldiers. Then, he saw one throw something.

Shit. The device landed in front of Smith's snowmobile and exploded.

His machine was tossed up into the air, tipping over. He leaped off, hit the snow, and rolled.

He came up on one knee, firing his CXM.

"Team 52, stop the artifact!" Lachlan shouted.

Smith's jaw tightened. He had a job to do, but where the hell was his woman?

He rose, racing to join his team. But in his head, her name echoed. *Kinsey, where the hell are you?*

CHAPTER SEVENTEEN

Enzo continued to drag Kinsey through the snow, but she wasn't making it easy for him. At every opportunity, she dug her boots in.

After a fast, wild snowmobile ride, he hadn't listened to any of her pleading. *Asshole.* Now, they'd abandoned the snowmobile, and he was pulling her up a hill. Gunfire cracked nearby, and she prayed Team 52 was close.

Snow seeped into her boots and she winced. She had a new appreciation for the desert. The cold sucked.

Finally, she saw something ahead. No, a someone.

She hissed out a breath. It was a man using the artifact. He stood, dressed in black winter gear, with his lips pressed to the end of the trumpet-like device.

The low, melodic hum of sound reverberated in Kinsey's ears. As she and Enzo got closer, the man using the artifact looked in their direction.

Dark brows moved low over even darker eyes. He glared at her, then Enzo. He was clearly annoyed.

Then Kinsey turned her head and looked down the hill. She gasped.

Below, lay the entrance to Cheyenne Mountain, and all around it, rocks, cars, and other objects were slamming down into the ground. Soldiers were running for cover, and closer, up on the snowy hill, she saw Team 52 in their white outfits, fighting against the Cosca Unita soldiers.

Chest tight, she scanned the landscape, searching for one big form in particular.

There. She spotted Smith wrestling with not one, but two, Cosca Unita fighters.

Then a giant rock went flying through the air. *Oh, no.* It was arrowing straight toward the entrance to the base.

Boom.

The man using the artifact paused, the sound abruptly cutting off.

He scowled at Enzo. "Why the fuck did you grab her?"

"She's mine, Angelo," Enzo said.

Kinsey snorted. "Am not. See that big guy pummeling your guys into the snow?" She pointed to Smith. "I'm in love with him. And he's going to rip your head off."

Enzo ground his teeth together. "I'll make you forget him."

She rolled her eyes. "Look at him. He's big, alpha, and a protective badass. And you're..." she eyed him and wrinkled her nose "...not."

"Focus," Angelo snapped. "This is no time to be

thinking with your damn cock. It's time to take these guys out, then we can focus on tearing the base apart."

"You're insane," Kinsey breathed.

Cold, dark eyes bored into her. "I'm dedicated. I have a vision where the powerful take what they deserve and the weak serve."

She shivered. There was a thirst for power in this man's gaze. She could see that no rational argument was going to sway him.

Angelo lifted the device and blew into it again.

Sound vibrated out, and this time, the ground around them started tearing up, snow flying into the air. Rocks ripped from the hillside, rising high. The ground beneath them shook.

The rocks flew, moving faster and faster...straight at Team 52.

"No! Stop!" Without thinking, Kinsey dived at the man.

He grunted and lost his grip on the artifact. The sound cut off.

"Kinsey." Enzo dived into the fray.

The three of them wrestled in the snow.

Angelo shoved Kinsey off and she looked up. She heard shouts. Smith was powering through the snow, his gaze locked on her, and behind him, several figures were sprinting up the hill toward them.

He was coming for her.

She smiled at him. Then, Angelo scrambled to grab the device again.

Hell, no. She had to stop him and protect Team 52.

She moved her gloved hand, brushing against a rock. Her fingers closed over it.

Angelo blew into the device, the sound starting again.

She might go to hell for damaging an ancient artifact, but oh, well. She raised the rock, then slammed it down on the device.

Clang.

She lifted the rock and did it again. And again.

The artifact's sound changed, losing its melodic resonance. All around, rocks dropped from the sky, like puppets that had had their strings cut.

Kinsey grinned. *Yes!*

Dark eyes glared at her. The man shoved the artifact away, and pulled a gun from his coat.

Oh, shit.

He aimed the weapon at her.

"Kinsey!" Smith yelled. But he was still too far away.

Kinsey heard the echo of the gunshot, just as she felt herself shoved down hard. She landed heavily in the snow, the air knocked out of her. A heavy weight pinned her to the ground.

She turned on her side and saw Enzo.

He was on top of her and he was bleeding. He pressed a hand to his chest, his eyes wide. She sucked in a breath. He'd taken a bullet for her.

Her throat closed. "It'll be okay." She pressed her hand against the bleeding wound, trying to stem the blood flow. "Hold on."

Angelo rose to his feet, and turned the weapon on Team 52. He fired and she watched as her friends all dived for cover.

But not Smith. He kept coming.

Angelo swiveled, aiming the gun right at Smith.

No. Kinsey couldn't lose him. She wouldn't lose him. She nudged Enzo aside and pushed herself up. She dived into Angelo's legs. He swiveled, falling. He cursed and swung the gun at her.

Bam.

Searing pain. Kinsey landed awkwardly in the snow, blinking. Bodies swarmed around them.

She saw Lachlan kick the gun out of Angelo's hand. He flipped the man over and wasn't gentle about it.

Kinsey tried to pull in a breath, but it hurt.

Then Smith was there, sliding to his knees at her side.

"It's okay, baby. I've got you."

God, he was so beautiful. He was tugging at her coat and vest with desperate hands.

She frowned. Her white coat was now red. *Weird.*

"Callie!" Smith roared. "Bastard was firing armor-piercing rounds."

A second later, the medic dropped down beside them. "Shit."

Smith's hands were pressing hard on Kinsey's stomach and she groaned in pain.

"Gut shot." Smith's voice was deep, harsh.

"Hurts." But strangely, Kinsey's pain was fading.

Smith's face appeared, an inch from hers. "Hold on, Kinsey."

She reached up and scratched her nails through his beard. "You make me feel safe."

"Hold. On."

But even though she wanted to hold him forever, Kinsey couldn't keep her eyelids open.

Smith's face became a blur, then nothing but black.

SMITH CARRIED Kinsey's limp form down the hill.

They were both covered in blood, Callie walking alongside them, trying to keep Kinsey stabilized.

"Fuck." Lachlan's face was grim as he touched his ear. "Brooks, we need to get Kinsey to the hospital ASAP. I need a helo here, now."

"On it," came Brooks reply.

"What about Enzo?" Callie called out.

Smith didn't give a fuck about the asshole.

"He didn't make it," came Blair's answer.

Smith sucked in some deep breaths, his gaze locked on Kinsey's pale face. He tried to keep a grip on the ugly sensations clawing at his gut.

Inside, he was cold. Frozen.

Kinsey was light and laughter, beauty and goodness. But right now, she was as white as the snow under his boots and bleeding badly. Her life blood was pumping out of her.

"Put her down," Callie said.

The medic dropped down, pulling things from her backpack. She pressed a new wad of gauze against Kinsey's belly, and then cut the sleeve off Kinsey's coat. She set up an IV.

"Pickup is incoming," Brooks said.

"Hold on, sunshine." Smith didn't wonder how

Brooks managed to pull off a helicopter pickup so quickly. He kept his gaze on Kinsey, couldn't look away.

Kinsey was everything. Without her, Smith knew there'd be no light in his life

Lachlan gripped Smith's shoulder. "You hanging in there?"

"She's hurt bad." Smith heard the tremor in his own voice.

"We're going to take care of her. She's a fighter."

"I screwed up with her." Pain tore at Smith. "I pushed her away. I knew she was special and I pushed her away. Wasted so much time."

"She loves you," Lachlan said.

God. It seemed like a miracle. And hell, Smith loved her, too. He'd tear his heart from his chest and hand it to her, if that's what it took to save her life.

Thwap, thwap, thwap. Hearing the sound of helicopter rotors, he looked up.

Snow kicked up around them, and he saw the sleek helo coming in to land. He spotted Dec and Cal Ward in the cockpit.

"You, Callie, and Axel take her in," Lachlan said. "The rest of us will finish the cleanup here, talk to NORAD, and then we'll meet you at the hospital as soon as we can."

Smith nodded, scooping Kinsey off the ground, and carrying her into the helicopter.

"Hold on, baby."

Smith laid Kinsey down on the seats at the back of the helicopter.

Dec looked back at him from the cockpit, lifting his headset off his ears. "How bad?"

Callie climbed in. "Bad."

That single word speared through Smith. He felt parts of him closing down inside.

"Fuck," Dec said. "Then strap in."

Callie checked Kinsey's wound. "Talk to her, big guy. She needs to hear your voice."

Smith nodded, threading his fingers through Kinsey's limp ones. God, her hands were small, her fingers delicate.

Axel sat down in the seat across from them, his CXM resting on his knees, and a grim look on his face. He watched Smith steadily, probably for any signs he was going to lose his shit.

The helo rose and Smith sucked in a breath. Finding some shred of control, he stroked Kinsey's short hair.

"I remember the first time I saw you," he murmured. "You knocked the breath out of me. You were so damn pretty. I remember you were wearing a pink T-shirt." He smiled at the memory. "I'd always hated pink, but right then, I'd never seen a prettier color. Then you smiled at me. You have the most beautiful smile, Kinsey. I think that's when I first started falling for you."

He glanced up. Callie and Axel were staring at him.

"Don't let her die." His voice was like sandpaper.

Callie bit down on her lip and nodded.

Then Smith looked back down at Kinsey's still face. He kept murmuring to her, telling her all the things he loved about her. How she made his life brighter.

It felt like forever, but finally, the helicopter came in to land on the roof of a hospital.

As Axel opened the side door, an emergency team raced to meet them, pushing a gurney. Kinsey was taken from Smith's arms, and as they whisked her away, Smith moved to follow.

Axel grabbed his arm and Smith barely controlled his snarl.

"Let them do their jobs, big guy."

Gritting his teeth, Smith stood there, feeling totally helpless. He watched the team move out of sight. With Kinsey gone, Smith felt like someone had turned off the lights.

LIGHTS. Voices. Movement.

Kinsey blinked slowly, watching the blur of the ceiling and lights. She blinked again, the movement feeling like it took about a year.

Where was Smith? She wanted Smith.

She had a mask on her face, and someone in blue scrubs leaned over her. The woman's mouth was moving, but Kinsey just heard a drone of sound.

Pain hit her, shooting through her body. *Oh, boy, her belly hurt. Really bad.*

Smith. Where was he?

"You're in the hospital," someone said. "Relax. We're taking good care of you."

Kinsey blinked again. The darkness was calling her again. And there was no pain there.

But there was also no Smith...

She struggled, trying to raise her arms, trying to speak. She fought to keep her eyelids open, but this was a battle she was destined to lose.

Soon, there was nothing but the dark.

CHAPTER EIGHTEEN

S mith sat on the uncomfortable chair in the hospital waiting room. He hadn't moved for a long time, just stared blindly at the floor.

They'd been there for hours. Kinsey had been in surgery all that time.

Blair sat down beside him and slid her arm through his.

"She's a fighter, Smith. First time I saw her, I thought Jonah was joking, hiring this pretty, sweet wannabe-showgirl."

Yeah, a part of Smith had thought the same thing. And another part of him had been reeling from her beauty and the promise of her.

Something in him had known, had recognized what she'd be to him.

Now, she was lying somewhere in a hospital operating room, cut open, fighting for her life.

"But then I saw how smart she was," Blair continued.

"How organized. She was out to prove she could do the job, and she was right. She's damn good at it." A smile tilted Blair's lips. "Half the time, she maneuvers us without us even knowing."

It was all true. And Kinsey did all of it with that megawatt smile on her face. It was just another reason Smith was crazy about her.

He looked down at his hands. He'd washed them, but there was still some blood caked around his nails.

Kinsey's blood.

"I didn't protect her. I didn't keep her safe."

"You did," Blair said. "And you did more than that. You trusted her. You let Kinsey be Kinsey, and do her part to help. She's talked a little bit about her life before... and it sounds like she's never had that." Blair patted his thigh. "You trusted Kinsey to protect herself, to be a part of this mission, to do something important."

Smith lifted his head, looking at his friend. Emotion was a hard, painful ball in his chest.

"And you let her protect you," Blair said. "The man she loves."

He pulled in a shaky breath.

"Who's here for Kinsey Beck?" a voice called out.

Smith pushed to his feet, his gaze going straight to the tired-looking female doctor wearing blue scrubs. Throat tight, he felt his team moving in around him.

"She's mine," Smith said. "Kinsey's mine."

The doctor gave a faint smile. "Then you're a lucky man. She is a hell of a fighter, and she pulled through surgery just fine."

Smith's shoulders sagged. God. *God.* "Can I see her?"

"Soon. I'll let you know when you can go back."

As the doctor nodded and turned away, Smith felt like someone had turned the lights in his life back on.

His friends slapped him on the back.

Kinsey was going to be okay. She was okay.

***

Blair

BLAIR MASON WATCHED through the doorway as Smith sat beside Kinsey's bed.

The big man was murmuring quietly, and even though Kinsey looked small and pale propped up on the pillows, she was smiling.

It wasn't her usual beaming smile, but it was something.

Thank God. Kinsey was fine and Smith looked alive again.

During the tense hours in the waiting room, Smith had been like a statue—cold and still. His brown eyes had been devoid of...everything.

Blair watched as he leaned over and kissed Kinsey.

Jesus. Blair felt her heart clench. They were so damn cute together. Smith was a big, tough guy. Blair had fought alongside him so many times, and trusted him with her life. She knew he loved his solitude and his cabin near the mountains. Knew he loved nothing more than the serene beauty of the Colorado mountains.

She never, ever imagined seeing him like this. In love.

Blair had watched three of her teammates—three of

the toughest guys she knew—fall in love. First Lachlan, then Seth, and now Smith. They were all unashamed to show how they felt about the women who'd captured their hearts.

Blair had always thought she wanted that. A man who loved her inside and out, for exactly who she was, and wasn't afraid to show it.

And yet... That kind of man was hard to find. And she'd spent the last few hours sitting in the waiting room down the hall, watching Smith being torn to shreds.

Maybe love wasn't all it was cracked up to be.

"You called it." Lachlan appeared beside her. "The bigger they are..."

"Yeah." Blair pushed her maudlin thoughts away. Besides, she'd never met a man who made her feel anything remotely close to love. In fact, most men—after a quick, pleasant tussle—annoyed her.

Anyway, she had zero time to date. She couldn't really share the truth of her work with a man, and she found most guys...kinda boring.

"The artifact?" she asked Lachlan.

Her best friend lifted his chin. "All packed up. Seth's guarding it at the X8 until we're ready to head home. It's beaten up. Arlo and Ty are going to have a shit hemorrhage."

"Ty will fix it." Blair paused. "So, another mission over."

"Yeah. The military police from Cheyenne Mountain took all the surviving Cosca Unita people into custody. Mission's over and we can go home."

For Lachlan now, home meant his woman, Rowan. Blair was happy as hell for him.

Lachlan's golden gaze moved to Smith and Kinsey. "Could have done without Kinsey taking a bullet to the gut, though."

"She's okay."

"Yeah. And so is Smith."

"Well, once we get home, we'll have to enjoy some downtime before we need to save the world again," Blair said.

Lachlan tossed an arm around her shoulders. He'd been her best friend for years, from their time in Force Recon. Why were all the best men she knew her friends and colleagues? Guys who were like brothers to her?

"You won our last poker game," Lachlan said, interrupting her thoughts. "I want a chance to win some money back."

Blair grinned. "No such luck. You are going down, Hunter."

He smiled back.

Blair kept her smile plastered on her face. She had good friends and work she loved. She didn't need a man.

SMITH STRODE THROUGH THE BASE, happy to finish their training exercises for the day. He was eager to get home to Kinsey.

It had been three weeks since she'd been shot. Three weeks since they'd come home to Las Vegas.

She'd spent that time recuperating at his cabin. He

smiled. Just that morning, he'd left her tucked up in his bed with Hercules. She'd mumbled a good bye, but his Kinsey took at least an hour to wake up and join the land of the living.

Smith knew she was itching to get back to work. He strode into the rec room and moved to the refrigerator. He knew she was getting close to being ready to go back to the Bunker, but he wanted to be absolutely sure she was fit and healthy.

He pulled a drink out of the fridge.

"Hey." Ty's voice made him turn around and lift his chin.

The scientist and Arlo were carrying a big, black box. They set it on one of the tables, and Ty flicked open the lid.

The Tibetan artifact lay inside, nestled in black foam.

"What are you guys up to?"

"I've been repairing the horn." Ty gave it another close look, then shut the lid. "It's all back to normal."

"Did you test it?" Smith asked.

Ty's lips quirked. "Oh yeah."

Apparently, he'd had fun doing it.

"Did you work out why it doesn't levitate people?" Smith asked.

Ty nodded. "This particular artifact produces the right kind of standing waves to levitate solid objects, but not organic things. Sonic levitation of humans is possible, just not with this artifact."

"Well, I'll tell Kinsey you fixed it," Smith said. "She's had a few nightmares about destroying an ancient artifact."

Ty smiled, his teeth white against his darker skin. Arlo grunted.

"How is she doing?" Ty asked.

"A whole lot better." Smith checked her wound daily, much to her annoyance. It was healing up nicely and she was getting around the cabin easily.

He glanced at his watch. And now he was extra keen to get back to his woman.

"You take good care of your gal, Creed," Arlo said. "No more kidnappings or gunshot wounds."

Hell, Smith hoped not. "Doing that, Arlo."

Arlo hefted the box, nodded at them, and left. He'd be heading back to the secure warehouse to store the artifact.

Where the damn thing couldn't hurt anyone.

Soon, Smith met the rest of his team by the elevator. Like him, everyone was showered and wearing civilian clothes. They moved on autopilot, boarding the X8, and taking off.

Smith napped on the trip back to Las Vegas, and at the airport, he waved to the others. Then he aimed his truck in the direction of his cabin. He made a couple of quick stops on the way.

The sun was setting as he pulled up in front of his place. Lights were on inside.

Damn, he liked that. He enjoyed his own company, but he also loved having Kinsey in his space. In their home. She brightened up everything.

Smith knew now that he loved the sunshine. He loved walking in it.

When he pushed open the door to the cabin, a delicious smell hit him. Hercules rushed to greet him with a woof. Smith dropped his duffel bag and rubbed his dog's head, his gaze going to Kinsey in the kitchen.

God. He loved this.

She was wearing leggings and a T-shirt. She'd had her hair cut into a short style and while he missed the long locks, it looked cute tousled around her face. She looked up and smiled.

"Hey," he said.

"You're home." She made a beeline for him, smiling.

Kinsey went to leap on Smith, but he stopped her, gripping her hips. He was worried about her wound.

Her bright smile faded, and he dropped his head to press a quick kiss to her lips. "What's for dinner?"

"Chili."

"Got something for you." He held up the small paper bag he held.

She peered in, her lips quirking. "Another candle-making kit."

"Saw you were nearly out of wax."

"If I make any more candles, we won't be able to move in here."

She'd spread the colorful candles all around the cabin —in the bedroom, on the mantel above the fire place, hell, even in the bathroom. Smith liked seeing them everywhere.

"Let me dump my gear and wash up."

She nodded, but his gut tightened.

Most of the time, Kinsey seemed fine. Perfectly recovered from her injury and the mission. But then her light would sometimes dim. He'd see her eyes turn dull, thoughts churning behind her blue eyes.

She turned away from him. His dog butted against her legs, and she gave him a rub, talking nonsense to him. Damn dog was practically hers now.

Smith headed for the bedroom, his jaw tight. After dumping his bag and washing his hands, he headed back into the kitchen.

She was stirring the chili and he stared at her slim back.

Something was bothering her, and he was going to find out what.

KINSEY BRUSHED HER TEETH, getting ready for bed. Hercules sat on the bathmat beside her. It had become their ritual. The handsome dog loved keeping her company whenever she brushed her teeth.

They'd eaten her chili, and it had been delicious, even if she did say so herself. Smith had sipped on a beer and she'd had a glass of wine.

Now, all she wore were her panties and one of Smith's T-shirts. Rinsing and setting her brush down, she lifted the hem of the shirt, baring her cute, green, boy-leg panties and her belly.

She fingered the scar on her skin. It wasn't very pretty.

But she was breathing.

Every day, she reminded herself that she'd made it.

She'd helped stop Cosca Unita, kept people safe, and she'd protected Team 52.

She dropped the shirt down and looked back in the mirror.

And tonight, she was breaking up with Smith.

She nibbled her lip, pain rolling through her. It was time to go home. Time to get back to work. Time to stop pretending.

Once things were back to normal, she could start putting together the pieces of her shattered heart.

Since Colorado, Smith hadn't touched her. Holding her close on the couch, yes. A quick kiss when they woke, or when he left for work, sure. Sleeping with his arms wrapped around her, every night.

But he hadn't made love to her. She swallowed.

She wasn't in danger anymore, and he didn't need to protect her any longer. And it appeared that he didn't want her the way she wanted him. Growing up in that trailer in Tennessee, Kinsey had been forced to settle for less.

She set her shoulders back. Not this time. Not even when she was tempted to have a slice of Smith any way he came.

Rubbing Hercules' head, she fought back the despair carving out her insides. "I'll miss you, boy." Her words were a whisper.

When she exited the bathroom, Smith was standing beside the big bed, silhouetted by the window behind him.

He was naked.

Kinsey's mouth went dry. She barely noticed

Hercules darting out of the bedroom. She watched Smith toss his jeans on a chair. He was still the most beautiful man she'd ever seen. Her gaze raked up his body—from his prosthetic foot, up the powerful legs, past the thick cock, over the chiseled abs and chest.

He glanced up. "Ready for bed?"

She nodded, then she shook her head.

He frowned. "Is that a yes or no?"

She took a step forward, then stopped. She clutched her hands together.

He sat down on the bed, frowning at her. "Kinsey?"

"I'm going home tomorrow."

He stiffened, his gaze sharpening on her.

"I'm all healed. I'm safe." Her voice cracked, but she sucked in a breath. "I spoke with my sister and she's going to stop by and help me out if I need it." Another deep breath. "You're off duty now, Smith."

He just stared at her. "You want to leave?"

No. I want to stay with you forever. I want you to touch me, hold me, confess your undying love. "It's best if—"

"Not what I asked." His voice was hard, gruff.

She felt tears prick in her eyes. "Why are you making this hard? I thought you'd be happy. You don't want me here."

He stood so fast, she jolted. He stalked toward her like some mountain predator.

Kinsey backed up a few steps, but his long legs ate up the distance. She collided with his hard chest.

"Why do you think I don't want you here?"

She swallowed. "You...you don't need to protect me

anymore. And you don't want me...um, physically anymore."

He grabbed her hand and slid it lower. He pressed it over his cock. A very hard cock.

Reflexively, her fingers wrapped around him and her lips parted. Her belly spasmed.

"Never doubt how much I want you, Kinsey. It's been hell lying beside you, wanting you, but knowing you hadn't healed enough."

"That's why...?" God, he'd still been protecting her.

"You bring light to my world. I'd die for you, kill for you, and as long as I knew you were okay, I'd happily live with that."

It wasn't exactly hearts and flowers, but it was a hell of a macho-man declaration.

"Since I got shot, you haven't touched me. I just thought, since you haven't made love to me—"

Suddenly, she was lifted off her feet. She gasped and his mouth hit hers.

Smith was holding her, kissing her.

Pure need shot through Kinsey. She deepened the kiss, sliding her tongue against his. She wrapped her legs around his hips, undulating against him.

Then he pinned her against the wall. He made a hungry sound—part groan, part growl—and she felt a flood of damp between her legs. Then his hands were tearing at her clothes. He yanked the shirt up over her head, and then with one violent tug, he tore her panties off.

Oh, God. If she hadn't been drenched before, she was now.

His gaze collided with hers, locked. He shifted her up and then he thrust inside her.

Their groans mingled.

He started moving, thrusting hard. Kinsey clutched him, surging against him with every thrust. She kept her eyes locked with his. Staring at the emotion boiling in his eyes.

Soon she was panting and his breathing was fast, hard pants. Sensation poured through her—hot, beautiful, amazing. His thrusts got harder, sharper.

"Smith!"

"You're close." His voice was guttural. "Come, sunshine."

A soul-shattering orgasm hit her. Kinsey let out a cry, pressing her face into his neck. Everything she felt for him mixed with the pleasure, pouring through her in a hot rush.

Smith thrust deep, staying there as a harsh groan ripped out of him. She stroked his back, feeling small shivers running through him.

Kinsey let out a long, happy breath. She was wrapped up in Smith's arms. Safe, satiated, secure.

His lips hit her ear. "I've been waiting for you to heal."

"I'm healed." She clutched his big shoulders.

"I've been waiting for you to let me know."

God. She bit down on his bottom lip, pressing into him. "I should have said something."

He nuzzled her neck. "I should have explained better."

"I guess we need to work on our communication

since I can't read your subtle mountain man clues, and you don't talk much." She stroked his beard. "I was scared."

He lifted his head. "You're safe with me, Kinsey. You can tell me anything, ask me anything, any time."

"Okay." She paused. "Smith, will you fuck me again? Please?"

He gave her one of his sexy half smiles. So gorgeous. "No."

She blinked. "No?"

"I'll make love to you."

Warmth filled her chest. As he kissed her again, she let her hands roam over him. He pulled out of her, then spun, carrying her to the bed. He laid her down like she was something precious.

His fingers ran over her, exploring every inch of her skin. He worshiped her with his hands, then added his mouth. His lips traveled down her body until she was writhing beneath him.

When he reached her scar, she stiffened.

"I didn't hurt you?"

"Not a bit," she answered.

His lips moved gently over her scar, and he took his time. Slowly, she relaxed.

"It's a badge of honor, babe."

She stared into his face, and all she saw was need and desire.

"You match the rest of us on the team now," he added. "We all have our scars."

She smiled, and then his head moved lower. When his very talented mouth moved between her legs, she arched into him. She slid her hands into his hair and gave herself up to the way this man made her feel. Like she was flying.

After she'd splintered apart, and cried out his name while she did it, he moved back up. With a single thrust, he was inside her.

Then, there were no more thoughts, only glorious feeling.

CHAPTER NINETEEN

Lying on his back, Smith smiled at the ceiling. Kinsey rested on top of him, her face tucked into his neck. She hadn't moved since she'd come a third time.

His cock was still inside her, and he lazily stroked her back, feeling pretty damn content. He could happily stay like this for the rest of his life.

"So, you aren't leaving," he finally said.

"I'm not leaving."

"You'll stay here with me."

She looked up, her eyes sexy, her hair rumpled. "Yes. I really like your dog," she teased.

Smith smiled. "I want you to move in."

Her blue eyes went wide and her smirk disappeared.

"It's a longer commute," he said. "But when I'm not here, you'll have Hercules for company."

She blinked. "You want me to move in?"

He slid his hands into her hair. God, it always felt like silk. "Yeah."

"Together?"

He smiled. "I don't think you're quite following what's going on here."

"Well, we're in bed..."

He pulled her closer. His sweet Kinsey. He realized now that she lived for the moment, enjoying the hell out of the now. What she didn't do was let herself dream, and imagine things for the future.

Smith was going to help her with that. Help her learn to fly. Whatever she wanted, he'd bleed to give it to her.

"You're it for me, Kinsey. You move in, and then when we're ready, I'll find a ring that suits you. Diamonds, maybe some of those pink ones."

Her mouth dropped open, her breaths coming sharp and fast. She just stared at him.

Smith sat up, bringing her with him.

"Whatever kind of wedding you want, big, small, or if you want to elope, we'll do it. As long as you're there, I don't care. And down the track, I hope you want some kids." Imagining her swollen with their child made his gut tighten.

"You want to marry me?" she said breathlessly.

"Yes."

"You want babies? With me?"

"Yes, sunshine. I want to make a life with you. Forever."

She tilted her head. "Why?"

Fuck her parents. They'd scarred things in her, and if he ever met them...

"Because you're beautiful, smart, sweet, and caring. You light up a room. And because I love you."

ANNA HACKETT

Her hands convulsed on him, her eyes glimmering with unshed tears. "You love me?"

He cupped her jaw. "Yeah, sunshine. I've been trying to show you that by taking care of you."

"I love you, too," she said.

He smiled. He already knew the way she felt about him. It was written all over her pretty face whenever she looked at him. But it felt damn good to hear her say the words. "Happy to hear that, babe."

"And Smith?"

"Yeah?"

"I *need* the words."

"I love you, Kinsey. Say it a hundred times a day, if you want me to."

She cupped his cheeks. "You, big, beautiful, sexy Smith Creed love me, Kinsey Mae Beck."

"Guys are not beautiful."

"You are. To me."

To shut her up, he closed his mouth over hers. Her lips parted instantly and she shifted closer to him. His Kinsey, always so hungry for him.

Smith raised his head. "I got something for you." He set her aside and strode over to his duffel bag.

"You've already given me the best thing ever," she said.

He looked back at her with a grin. "Orgasms?"

She smiled and rolled her eyes. "Those were good. But no, I meant your heart. I've only ever wanted you, Smith. A good man, a protective man. One who loves me back."

His throat tightened. Hell, she slayed him. He moved back toward the bed. "These are for you."

She stared at the bunch of yellow flowers in his hand, a stunned look on her face.

"You got me flowers?"

They were slightly wilted, since he'd forgotten about them in his bag. He sat beside her and pressed them into her hand. "I'll get you flowers every week for the rest of our lives, if that makes you happy."

She took the flowers, stroking the petals. "All I want is you."

"Whatever you want, I'll get it for you, Kinsey."

Her smile turned downright sexy. She pressed a hand to his chest, smoothing it downward. "And what if I want to seduce the man I love?"

Smith let her push him back against the pillows. "Then I'm all yours."

KINSEY SAT CONTENTEDLY at the bar in Griffin's. She popped a fry into her mouth.

They were having a mini-celebration, as she was all moved into Smith's cabin. Today, the team had helped her shift her things and clear out her apartment.

She now lived with Smith Creed—the man who loved her and wanted to marry her one day—and she couldn't be happier.

Blair, also eating fries, caught her eye and winked.

Kinsey grinned. Yep, she was on top of the world.

Right here, she was surrounded by people who cared about her.

She turned her head, looking at Smith, who was sitting beside her and sipping his beer. *God.* As she watched him drink, his strong throat working, her girly parts spasmed.

"Quit drooling, girl." Callie leaned in close from Kinsey's other side.

Kinsey just grinned at her. She finally had it all. Work she loved, good friends, and the man of her dreams. She, Kinsey Mae Beck from Sugarview, Tennessee, had it all.

Sorry, Ma. You were wrong.

"I'm heading to the ladies room." Kinsey slipped off her stool.

Smith reached out and stroked her hair. She tossed him a smile and headed to the restroom. When she returned, Axel, Callie, Blair, and Seth were shooting pool in what looked like an extremely intense match. Blair was glaring at Axel, and Seth was scowling as he watched Callie take a shot. Man, these guys were so competitive.

"You're going down, Diaz," Blair said.

Axel swung his pool cue like a weapon. "You're dreaming, *chica.*"

Blair ducked the cue. "I'm gonna wipe the floor with your handsome ass."

Shaking her head, Kinsey headed back to the bar and Smith. As she approached, she noticed a tall brunette sauntering up to him.

Kinsey got close enough to hear the woman talking.

"Need some company, handsome?"

Smith gave her a closed look. "No."

"Come on. You hooked up with a friend of mine, once." The brunette lowered her voice. "You left her with some *very* good memories. I'd love a few of my own."

Oh, so *not happening.* Kinsey tapped the woman on the shoulder.

The brunette spun, a frown on her face.

"Sorry," Kinsey said. "But I get to make those memories now." She pointed at Smith. "Because he's mine."

"Really?" the brunette said, derisively.

"Really." Kinsey cocked a hip.

"Kinsey." Smith's voice was filled with amusement.

"So, off you go." Kinsey waved a hand, dismissing the woman.

The brunette's face went red. "Maybe he'll see something better and change his mind."

Kinsey took a step toward the woman, but Smith wrapped a hand around her waist and dragged her between his open legs.

"Nothing better to see than what I have right here," Smith drawled.

Kinsey tilted her head back and smiled at him. He touched his lips to hers.

"Love you, big guy."

"And I love you, sunshine."

The brunette made a choked noise, then turned on her heel and stomped off.

Smith's smile widened. "So, I'm yours, huh?"

"You sure are."

Nearby, Rowan and January clapped. Lachlan was shaking his head. Kinsey giggled.

"My badass girl," Smith murmured.

"I did help beat terrorists, leaped from a levitating truck, and got shot. I can totally deal with any woman who tries to steal my man."

Smith's smile dimmed. "You do not make jokes about jumping from vehicles and getting shot. Like ever again."

"Sure thing, big guy." Kinsey spun in his arms and kissed him hard.

SMITH TOOK a sip of his beer. The pool game had turned into a death match. Seth and Callie had bowed out, but Blair and Axel were still going at it.

Kinsey was nestled into him, watching the game with bemusement. He breathed deep, drawing in the scent of strawberries.

Beside him, he watched Lachlan lean down and kiss Rowan. Seth was on the other side of the couple, arguing with January about...something. Those two seemed to argue a lot, and clearly liked it. Even as they threw insults at each other, the pair were smiling.

Smith's gaze came back to Lachlan, and he got it now. Smith understood. The need to risk it all for someone. He knew it was all worth it for that person who made your demons rest and your soul feel easy.

Smith stroked Kinsey's hair, moving the strands through his fingers. He was looking forward to their forever. He was planning a trip back to Colorado so she could meet his mom and dad. She was nothing like what they'd imagined for him, but he also knew they'd love her.

Suddenly, there was a blare of sirens from outside. He turned his head, seeing all his team glance up. Several police cruisers raced past.

"Trouble," Lachlan murmured.

As long as Kinsey was safe, Smith was happy. He'd had his quota of his woman being kidnapped and shot at. Enough to last a lifetime.

The bar door opened and a tall man stepped inside. Smith stiffened. Detective MacKade scanned the place, his gaze landing on them at the bar and not moving.

Ah, hell. The detective started toward them, his long legs closing the distance fast.

Then the man's gaze swiveled to the left, landing on Blair at the pool table. She'd stopped playing to watch him, her feet spread, and the pool cue held up against her shoulder like a staff.

She stared at him with narrowed eyes.

Lachlan rose. "MacKade."

"Hunter."

"Something tells me you're not here for a beer."

"No." The detective rested a hand on the bar. "I need your help."

Tension filled the room. Smith knew something bad was going down.

Blair strode up. "Why would we want to help you?"

"Blair," MacKade said. "Friendly as always."

Smith squeezed Kinsey and rose behind her. "You helped us when Kinsey was snatched. You need help, you've got mine."

Lachlan lifted his chin. "I know we don't always see eye to eye—"

Blair stabbed a finger at MacKade, interrupting. "He argues about everything. He makes me do paperwork, in goddamn triplicate. Half the time, he stonewalls us—"

"And you often tear through my city, leaving a trail of destruction and dead bodies behind you. You can't expect me to be happy about that, especially when I'm the one who cleans up your messes and hides it behind the word classified."

Blair shoved her hands on her hips. "We save lives!"

"I know. And I run interference for you far more than you realize."

Blair's mouth snapped closed.

"And now I need your help." The detective's gaze moved, taking them all in. "All of you." But then he looked at Blair again. "To save lives."

Lachlan gripped Rowan's shoulder. "I have to go, baby." He pressed a kiss to her lips.

The redhead nodded. "Go."

"Hellcat," Seth murmured to January.

"Me and the peanut will hitch a ride with Rowan," January said.

Smith turned to Kinsey.

She smiled, giving him a full blast of her sunshine. "Hercules and I will keep the bed warm."

He touched his mouth to hers. *God.* It was so good to know that after whatever they were wading into, he'd be heading home to her.

"Go." She shoved him. "Go save the world."

Smith was still smiling as he followed his team and MacKade out of the bar.

Whatever was going on, he wanted to get this done, so he could get back to his woman.

———————

I hope you enjoyed Kinsey and Smith's story!

Team 52 will continue with Blair's story, *Mission: Her Defense*, as she sets out to work with Detective Luke MacKade. Coming early 2019.

For more action-packed romance, and for a peek at *Treasure Hunter Security* owner Declan Ward's action-packed story, read on for a preview of *Undiscovered*.

Don't miss out! For updates about new releases, action romance info, free books, and other fun stuff, sign up for my VIP mailing list and get your *free box set* containing three action-packed romances.

Visit here to get started: www.annahackettbooks.com

FREE BOX SET DOWNLOAD

JOIN THE ACTION-PACKED ADVENTURE!

PREVIEW: UNDISCOVERED

S he was hot, dusty, and she'd never felt better.

Dr. Layne Rush walked across her dig, her boots sinking into the hot Egyptian sand. Ahead, she saw her team of archeologists and students kneeling over the new section of the dig, dusting sand away with brushes and small spades, methodically uncovering a recently discovered burial ground.

To her left, the yawning hole in the ground where they'd started the dig was like a large mouth, ringed on one side by a wooden scaffold.

In there, below the sands, was a fantastic tomb, and Layne was only beginning to unravel its secrets.

She paused and drew in a breath of warm desert air. To the east lay the Nile, the lifeblood of Egypt. She swiveled and watched the red-orange orb of the sun sinking into the Western Desert sands. All around, the dunes glowed. It made her think of gold.

Excitement was a hit to her bloodstream. Only days ago, they'd discovered some stunning golden artifacts down in the excavation. She'd found the first one—a small ushabti funerary figurine that would have been placed there to serve the tomb's as-yet-unknown occupant in the afterlife. After that, her team had discovered jewelry, a golden scarab, and a small amulet of a dog-like animal.

Stars started appearing in the sky, like tiny pinpricks of light through velvet. She breathed in again. The most exciting thing was the strange inscriptions carved into the dog amulet.

They had mentioned Zerzura.

Oh, Layne really wanted to believe Zerzura existed—a fabulous lost oasis in the desert, filled with treasure. She smiled as she watched the night darkness shroud the dunes. Her parents had read her bedtime stories of Zerzura as a child.

Thoughts of her parents, and the hard punch of grief that followed, made Layne's smile disappear. Unfortunately, life had taught her that fairytales didn't exist.

She shook off the melancholy. She'd made a life for herself, a career, and spent most of her time off on adventures on remote dig sites. She'd held treasures in her hands. She shared her love of history with anyone who'd listen. She hoped that if her mom and dad were still alive, they'd be proud of what she'd achieved.

Layne made her way toward the large square tents set up for dealing with the artifacts. One was for storage and one for study.

"Hey, Dr. Rush."

Layne spotted her assistant, Piper Ross, trudging up the dune toward her. The young woman was smart, opinionated, and not afraid to speak her mind. Her dark hair was cut short, the tips colored purple.

"Hi, Piper."

The young woman grinned. "Give you a whip and you'd look like something out of a movie." Piper swept a palm through the air. "Dr. Rush, dashing female adventurer."

Layne rolled her eyes. "Don't start. I still haven't lived down that last interview I did." What Layne had thought was a serious article on archeology had morphed into a story that turned her into a damned movie character. They'd even Photoshopped a whip in her hand and a hat on her head. "How's that new eastern quadrant coming along?"

"Excellent." Piper stopped, swiping her arm across her sweaty forehead. "I've got it all documented and photographed, and the tape laid out. We're ready to start digging tomorrow morning."

"Well done." Layne was hoping the new area would yield some excellent finds.

"Well, I *am* insanely good at my job—that's why you hired me, remember?" Piper grinned.

Layne tapped her chin. "Was that it? I thought it was

because you kept me in a constant supply of Diet Coke and chocolate."

Piper snorted. "Here they call it Coke Light, remember?"

Layne screwed up her nose. "I remember. The damn stuff doesn't taste the same."

"Yes, you really have to suffer out here on these remote digs."

"Can the sarcasm, Ross. Or I might forget why I keep you around."

Piper laughed. "A few of us are heading into Dakhla for the evening. Want to come?"

Dakhla Oasis was a two-hour drive north-east of the dig site. A group of communities, including the main town of Mut, were centered on the oasis. It was also where most of their local workers came from, and where they got their supplies.

Layne shook her head. "No, but thanks for the offer. I want to spend a bit more time on the artifacts we found, and take another look at the tomb plans. The main burial chamber and sarcophagus have to be in there somewhere."

"Unless grave robbers got to it," Piper suggested.

Layne shook her head. "When that local boy discovered this place it was clearly undisturbed." In between the discovery that had made headlines and her university being awarded the right to dig, the Egyptian Ministry of Antiquities had kept tight security on the place. She knew the Ministry would have preferred to run the dig themselves, but they just didn't have the funding to run every dig in the country. "I'm going to find out who's buried here, Piper."

The younger woman shook her head. "Well, just remember, all work and no play makes Dr. Rush very boring and in need of getting laid."

Layne rolled her eyes. "I'll worry about my personal life, thanks for your concern."

Piper stuck her hand on her hip. "You haven't dated since Dr. Stevens."

Ugh. Just hearing her colleague's name made Layne's stomach turn over. Dr. Evan Stevens had been a colossal mistake. He was tall and handsome, in a clean-cut way that suited his academic career as a professor of the Classics and History.

He'd been nice, intelligent. They'd liked the same restaurants. The sex hadn't been stellar, but it was fine. Layne had honestly thought he was someone she could come to love. More than anything, Layne wanted it all—a career, to travel, a husband who loved her, and most importantly, a family of her own. She wanted the love she remembered her parents sharing. She wanted the career they'd only dreamed of for her.

Maybe that had blinded her to the fact that Evan was an asshole hiding in an expensive suit.

Layne waved a hand dismissively. "I've told you before, I don't want to hear that man's name."

"I know you guys had a bad breakup..."

Ha. Piper didn't know half of it. Evan had stolen some of Layne's research and passed it off as his own. And he'd had the gall to tell her she was bad in bed. Moron.

"Look, go," Layne said. "Head into the oasis, soak in the springs, relax. You've got a lot of work to do tomorrow in the hot sun."

Piper groaned. "Don't remind me."

But Layne could see the twinkle of excitement in the young woman's eye. Layne saw it in her own every day. Being on a dig was always like that. Uncovering a piece of history...she could never truly describe how it made her feel. To touch something that someone had made, used, and cherished thousands of years ago. To uncover its secrets and try to piece together where it fit into the story of the world. To see what they could learn from it that might help them understand more about humanity.

She found it endlessly fascinating. Best job in the world.

After waving Piper off, Layne headed to the storage tent. The canvas door was still rolled up and secured at the top. As she stepped inside, the temperature dropped a little. Now that the sun had set, the temperature would drop even more. Nights in the desert, even in spring, could be chilly. She'd need to get to the portable shower they had set up and rinse off before it got too cold.

She'd lost count of the number of digs she'd been on. In the jungle, in the desert, under cities, by the ocean. She didn't care where they were, she just loved the challenge and thrill of uncovering the past.

Layne flicked on the battery-powered lantern hanging on the side of the tent. Makeshift shelves lined the space. Most were bare, waiting for the treasures they had yet to discover. But the first shelf was lined with shards of pottery, faience amulets, and stone carvings.

But it was the locked box at the base of the shelf she was most interested in.

She quickly dialed in the code on the tumbler-style lock and lifted the lid.

God. She stroked the ushabti reverently, its gold surface glowing in the lantern-light. Her parents would have loved to have seen this. To know their daughter had been the one to find it.

The necklace was still in pieces, but back in their lab in Cairo, someone would piece it back together. The chunky golden scarab would fit perfectly in the palm of her hand. She carefully lifted the small, dog-like amulet. It was slightly smaller than the scarab, and the canine had a slender body like a greyhound, and a long, stiff tail that was forked at the end. She was sure this was a set-animal, the symbol of the Egyptian god, Seth. She stroked the hieroglyphs on the animal's body and the symbols that spelled Zerzura.

Unfortunately, none of the hieroglyphs here made sense. She'd spent hours working on them. They were gibberish.

There was a noise behind her. A scrape of a boot in sand.

She turned, wondering who else had stayed behind.

A fist collided with her face in a vicious blow.

Pain exploded through Layne's cheek and she tasted blood. The blow sent her sprawling into the sand, the set-animal carving falling from her fingers.

Layne couldn't seem to focus. She lay there, her cheek to the sand, trying to clear her head. Her face throbbed and she heard voices talking in Arabic.

A black boot appeared in her line of sight.

A hand reached down and picked up the set-animal.

She swallowed, trying to get her brain working. Then she heard another voice. Deep, cool tones with a clipped British accent that made her blood run cold.

"Move it. I want it done. Fast."

She saw more people come into view. They were all wearing black balaclavas.

They started grabbing the artifacts and stuffing them into canvas bags.

"No." In her head her cry came out loud and outraged. In reality, it was a hoarse whisper.

"Bag everything," the cold voice behind her said.

No. She wasn't letting these thieves steal the artifacts. This was *her* dig and these were her antiquities to safeguard.

She pushed up onto her hands and knees. "Stop." She swung around and kicked at the knee of the man closest to her.

He tipped sideways with a cry.

"Uh-uh." The man with the cold voice stepped into her view. All she saw were his shiny black boots. Before she could do anything else, a hand grabbed her hair and yanked her head back.

The pain made her grit her teeth. Tears stung her eyes. She twisted, trying to pull away from him.

"A spitfire. I do like a feisty woman. Shame I don't have time to play with you."

He was behind her and she couldn't see his face. She tried to jerk away but a hard fist slammed into her head again.

No, no, no. Her vision dimmed, the sound of the thieves' voices receded.

Everything went black.

***

DECLAN WARD STRODE into the warehouse, his boots echoing on the scarred concrete. Colorado sunlight streamed through the large windows which offered a fantastic view of downtown Denver.

He was gritty-eyed from lack of sleep, and he was still adjusting to being back on Mountain Time.

He'd gotten in from finishing a job in South East Asia sometime around midnight. He'd unlocked his apartment, stumbled in and stripped, and fallen facedown on his bed.

Now, he was headed to work.

Lucky for him, it paid to be one of the owners. He lived above the warehouse that housed the main offices of Treasure Hunter Security.

Most of the open-plan space that had been a flour mill in a previous life was empty. But at the far end it was a different story.

Flat screens covered the brick wall, all displaying different images and scrolling feeds. Some sleek desks were set up, all covered in high-end computers.

There was a small kitchenette tucked into one corner, and next to that sat some sagging couches that looked like they'd come from a charity shop or some college student's house. Just beyond those, near the large windows, were a pool table and an air hockey table.

"Dec? What are you doing here?"

A small, dark-haired woman popped up from her seat at one of the computers. As always, she was dressed stylishly in dark jeans, a soft red sweater the color of raspberries, and impossibly high heels.

"I work here," he said. "Actually, I own the place. Have the mortgage to prove it."

His sister came right up to him and threw her arms around him. He did the same and absorbed the non-stop energy that Darcy always seemed to emit. She'd never been able to sit still, even as a little girl.

"You just got back. You're supposed to have a week off." She patted his arms and frowned. She had the same gray eyes he did, but hers always seemed to look bluer than his.

"Finished the job, ready for the next one."

Her frown deepened, her hands landing on her hips. "You work too hard."

"Darce, I'm tired, and not really up for this rant this morning." She had this spiel down to a fine art.

She huffed out a breath. "Okay. But I'm not done. Expect an earful later."

Great. He tweaked her nose. He'd done it ever since she was a cute little girl in pigtails and dirt-stained clothes tagging around after him and their brother Callum. Dec knew she hated it.

"Hey, Dec. When did you get back?"

Dec clasped hands with one of his team. Hale Carter was a big man, topping Dec's six-foot-two by a couple of inches. He'd been a hell of a soldier, was a bit of a genius with anything mechanical, and a guy who managed to smile through it all. He had a wide smile and dark skin courtesy of his African American mother, and a handsome face that drew the ladies like flies.

But Dec knew the man had secrets too, dark ones. Hell, they all did. They'd all been to some terrible places with the SEAL teams. All had seen and done some things that left scars—both physical and mental.

Dec never pried. He offered jobs to the former soldiers who wanted to work—ones where they normally wouldn't get shot at while doing them—and he didn't ask them to reveal all their demons.

Some demons could never be vanquished. He felt his gut tighten. Dec had accepted that long ago.

"Got in last night. Nice to be home." But even as he said the words, Dec knew it wasn't true. He was already feeling the itch to be out, moving, doing something.

It had been two and a half years since he'd left the Navy and stopped heading into the world's worst war zones. Hell, he didn't leave—they'd booted him out. He'd just barely avoided a dishonorable discharge, but they'd wanted him gone anyway, and he didn't blame them.

He shoved his hands into the pockets of his jeans. In those two and a half years, he'd put together Treasure Hunter Security with his brother and sister, and he'd never looked back. Or at least, he tried not to.

Hale was one of their newest recruits and had fit right in.

Dec made his way to the kitchenette and poured a cup of coffee from the pot. Darcy would have made it, which meant it was barely drinkable, but it was black and strong and had caffeine, so it ticked the boxes.

He saw his best friend slouched on one of the couches, his boots on the scarred coffee table and his long legs cased in well-worn jeans. He was flicking a switchblade open and closed.

"Logan."

"Dec."

Logan O'Connor was another SEAL buddy, and the best friend Dec had ever had. They hadn't liked each other at first, but after a particularly brutal mission—followed by an equally brutal bar fight in the seedy backstreets of Bangkok where they had saved each other's backs—they'd formed a bond.

Logan was big as well, the rolled-up sleeves of his shirt showing off his muscled arms and tattoos. From the day they'd left the military, Logan had let his brown hair grow long and shaggy, and his cheeks were covered in scruff. He looked exactly how he was—dangerous and just a little wild.

His friend eyed Dec up and down, then raised a brow. "How was the job?"

"The usual."

Actually, the jobs were never the same, and you were never sure what was going to happen. Providing security to archeological digs, retrieving stolen artifacts, occasionally turning some bad guys over to the authorities, doing museum security, or running remote expeditions for crazy treasure hunters...it kept things interesting.

"Anyone shoot at you?"

The female voice came from over by the computers. Morgan Kincaid sat cross-legged on top of a table. She was one of the few females to pass the rigorous BUD/S training for the Navy SEALs. But when the Navy had refused to let her serve on the teams, she'd left.

The Navy's loss was Dec's gain. Morgan was tough, mean, and hell in a firefight. She was tall, kept her dark hair short, and had a scar down the left side of her face from a knife fight.

"Not this trip," Dec answered.

"Too bad," Morgan murmured.

"All right everyone, listen up." Darcy's voice echoed in the warehouse.

They all headed over to where Darcy stood in front of her screens. Logan and Hale dropped into chairs, Morgan stayed sitting on top of the table, and Dec pressed a hip to a desk and sipped his coffee.

"Where's Cal?" he asked.

"He flew out a few days ago on another job. An anthropologist got snatched by a local tribe in Brazil."

"Hate the jungle," Logan said, his voice a growl.

"And Ronin?" Dec asked.

Ronin Cooper was another full-time Treasure Hunter Security employee. Dec kept a small full-time team and hired on trusted contractors when he needed more muscle.

"Coop's in northern Canada on an expedition."

Dec raised his brows, trying to imagine Ronin in the snow.

Hale hooted with laughter. "Shit, not too many shadows to hide in when you're in the snow."

Dec sipped his coffee again. Ronin Cooper was good at blending into the shadows. You didn't see him coming unless he wanted you to. Another former SEAL, Ronin had gotten out earlier than Dec, and had done some work for the CIA. Lean and intense, Ronin was the scary danger no one saw coming.

Dec settled back against the desk. "What's this new job?"

"An archeological dig in Egypt got attacked yesterday." Darcy pointed a small remote at her screens. A map of Egypt appeared with a red dot out in the Western Desert. "It's being run by the Rhodes University out of Massachusetts."

Dec raised a brow. Rhodes had a hell of an archeological department. They had their fingers in digs all over the world and prided themselves on some of the biggest finds in recent times. Every kid with dreams of being the next Indiana Jones wanted to study at Rhodes.

"The dig is excavating a newly-discovered tomb and surrounding necropolis," Darcy continued. "They'd recently found some artifacts." She pointed again and some images of artifacts appeared. "All gold."

Hale whistled. "Nice."

Dec's muscles tensed. He knew what was coming.

"And now the artifacts are gone." Darcy leaned back on the desk. "The head of the dig was working on the artifacts at the time and was attacked. She survived. And now, we're hired. One, to ensure no more artifacts are stolen, two to ensure the safety of the dig's workers, and three—" Darcy's blue-gray gaze met Dec's "—to recover the stolen artifacts."

Dec felt a muscle tick in his jaw. "It's Anders."

"Ah, hell." Logan tipped his head back. "This is not good."

Hale was frowning. "Who's Anders?"

"Dec has a hard-on for the guy," Morgan muttered.

Dec ignored Logan and Morgan. "Ian Anders. A former British Special Air Service soldier."

Hale's frown deepened. "Heard those SAS guys are hard-core."

"They are," Dec confirmed.

Darcy stepped forward. "Declan and Logan's SEAL team was working a joint mission with Anders' team in the Middle East."

"Caught the sadistic fucker torturing locals." Even now, the screams and moans of those people came back to Dec. A nightmare he couldn't seem to outrun. "He kept them hidden, visited them every few days. Men, women...children." Dec let out a breath. "No idea how long he'd had them there."

"You saved them?" Hale said.

"No." Dec stood and took his mug to the sink. He tipped the coffee he could no longer stomach down the drain.

"You did the right thing, Dec," Logan growled.

Silence fell. Dec was not going to talk about this.

Darcy cleared her throat. "The British Military gave Anders a slap on the wrist."

"Shit," Hale said. "So what's he got to do with stolen artifacts?"

"When he left the SAS, he got into black-market antiquities," Declan said. "We've run into him a few times on jobs."

"The guy is whacked," Logan added. "He likes to

hurt and kill. And he likes the pretty cash he gets for selling artifacts."

"And you think this is his work?" Hale looked at the screens.

Dec had learned to trust his gut. Sometimes despite the facts or evidence, despite the fact you had nothing else to go on. "Yeah, it's Anders."

"Logan, Morgan, and Hale, this is your assignment," Darcy said. "You'll head to Egypt to meet Dr. Layne Rush."

Another screen filled with a photo of a woman.

Dec blinked, feeling his belly clench, even though he'd never seen this woman before.

He wasn't even sure what warranted the gut-deep response. She was attractive, but not the most beautiful woman he'd ever seen. In the photo, she had sunglasses pushed up on her dark hair. Her hair was chocolate brown and straight as a ruler. It brushed her shoulders, except for the bangs cut bluntly just across her eyes. Her skin was so incredibly clear, not a blemish on it, and her eyes were hazel.

She had smart stamped all over her. *Hell.* Dec had a thing for smart women.

But he usually steered well clear. He wasn't made for hearts and rainbows. He'd just seen too much and done too much. His relationships generally lasted one night, and he enjoyed women who wanted the same as him— uncomplicated, no-strings sex.

"I'm going." Dec's voice echoed in the warehouse.

Darcy's beautiful face got a pinched look. "Declan—"

"No arguments, Darce. I'm going."

"You're going because of Anders," she said.

Dec glanced at the photo of Dr. Rush. "I'm going to pack."

His sister sighed and looked at Dec. "You're sure you won't change your mind."

"Nope."

Another sigh. "The jet's fueled and waiting. Logan, please keep him out of trouble."

Logan snorted. "I'm good, but I'm not that good."

Darcy shook her head. "All of you, have a good trip... and stay safe. Please."

Dec smiled, trying to break the tension. "You know me."

A resigned look crossed her face. "Yes. Unfortunately, I do. So when the trouble hits, call me."

Treasure Hunter Security

Undiscovered

Uncharted

Unexplored

Unfathomed

Untraveled

Unmapped

Unidentified

Undetected

PREVIEW - HELL SQUAD: MARCUS

READY FOR ANOTHER?

IN THE AFTERMATH OF AN ALIEN INVASION:

**HEROES WILL RISE...
WHEN THEY HAVE
SOMEONE TO LIVE FOR**

In the aftermath of a deadly alien invasion, a band of survivors fights on...

In a world gone to hell, Elle Milton—once the darling of the Sydney social scene—has carved a role for herself as the communications officer for the toughest commando team fighting for humanity's survival—Hell Squad. It's her chance to make a difference and make up for horrible past mistakes...despite the fact that its battle-hardened commander never wanted her on his team.

When Hell Squad is tasked with destroying a strategic alien facility, Elle knows they need her skills in the field. But first she must go head to head with Marcus Steele and convince him she won't be a liability.

Marcus Steele is a warrior through and through. He fights to protect the innocent and give the human race a chance to survive. And that includes the beautiful, gutsy Elle who twists him up inside with a single look. The last thing he wants is to take her into a warzone, but soon they are thrown together battling both the alien invaders and their overwhelming attraction. And Marcus will learn just how much he'll sacrifice to keep her safe.

Hell Squad

Marcus

Cruz

Gabe

Reed

Roth

Noah

Shaw

Holmes

Niko

Finn

Theron

Hemi

Ash

Levi

Manu
Also Available as Audiobooks!

ALSO BY ANNA HACKETT

Team 52

Mission: Her Protection

Mission: Her Rescue

Mission: Her Security

Also Available as Audiobooks!

Treasure Hunter Security

Undiscovered

Uncharted

Unexplored

Unfathomed

Untraveled

Unmapped

Unidentified

Undetected

Also Available as Audiobooks!

Galactic Gladiators

Gladiator

Warrior

Hero

Protector

Champion

Barbarian

Beast

Rogue

Guardian

Cyborg

Imperator

Also Available as Audiobooks!

Hell Squad

Marcus

Cruz

Gabe

Reed

Roth

Noah

Shaw

Holmes

Niko

Finn

Theron

Hemi

Ash

Levi

Manu

Also Available as Audiobooks!

The Anomaly Series

Time Thief

Mind Raider

Soul Stealer

Salvation

Anomaly Series Box Set

The Phoenix Adventures

Among Galactic Ruins

At Star's End

In the Devil's Nebula

On a Rogue Planet

Beneath a Trojan Moon

Beyond Galaxy's Edge

On a Cyborg Planet

Return to Dark Earth

On a Barbarian World

Lost in Barbarian Space

Through Uncharted Space

Crashed on an Ice World

Perma Series

Winter Fusion

A Galactic Holiday

Warriors of the Wind

Tempest

Storm & Seduction

Fury & Darkness

Standalone Titles

Savage Dragon

Hunter's Surrender

One Night with the Wolf

For more information visit AnnaHackettBooks.com

ABOUT THE AUTHOR

I'm a USA Today bestselling author and I'm passionate about **action romance**. I love stories that combine the thrill of falling in love with the excitement of action, danger and adventure. I'm a sucker for that moment when the team is walking in slow motion, shoulder-to-shoulder heading off into battle. I write about people overcoming unbeatable odds and achieving seemingly impossible goals. I like to believe it's possible for all of us to do the same.

My books are mixture of action, adventure and sexy romance and they're recommended for anyone who enjoys fast-paced stories where the boy wins the girl at the end (or sometimes the girl wins the boy!)

For release dates, action romance info, free books, and other fun stuff, sign up for the latest news here:

Website: www.annahackettbooks.com

Printed in Great Britain
by Amazon